G R JORDAN

Exit Stage Right

A Highlands and Islands Detective Thriller #50

First edition

ISBN (print): 978-1-917497-40-4
ISBN (digital): 978-1-917497-39-8

This book was professionally typeset on Reedsy.
Find out more at reedsy.com

I see retirement as just another of these reinventions, another chance to do new things and be a new version of myself.

Walt Mossberg

Contents

Foreword

The events of this book, while based around real and also fictitious locations around the UK, are entirely fictional and all characters do not represent any living or deceased person. All companies are fictitious representations and locations have been modified for the purposes of the story. This novel is best read from the stalls as you let the drama of the day slide away to be replaced by the stage before you!

Acknowledgments

To Ken, Jean, Colin, Evelyn, John and Rosemary for your work in bringing this novel to completion, your time and effort is deeply appreciated. And to everyone over the last 50 books in the the series who has encouraged, supported, read, and championed the writing, thank you all! You are just brilliant!

Books by G R Jordan

Seoras Macleod Mysteries

1. Seoras, They Shot Him! (Jan 2026)
2. Seoras, Grab the Kid! (Feb 2026)
3. Seoras, White Smoke Ahead! (Apr 2026)

The Highlands and Islands Detective series (Crime)

1. Water's Edge
2. The Bothy
3. The Horror Weekend
4. The Small Ferry
5. Dead at Third Man
6. The Pirate Club
7. A Personal Agenda
8. A Just Punishment
9. The Numerous Deaths of Santa Claus
10. Our Gated Community
11. The Satchel
12. Culhwch Alpha
13. Fair Market Value
14. The Coach Bomber

Kirsten Stewart Thrillers (Thriller)

Jac Moonshine Thrillers

1. Jac's Revenge
2. Jac for the People
3. Jac the Pariah

Siobhan Duffy Mysteries

1. A Giant Killing
2. Death of the Witch
3. The Bloodied Hands
4. A Hermit's Death

The Contessa Munroe Mysteries (Cozy Mystery)

1. Corpse Reviver
2. Frostbite
3. Cobra's Fang

The Patrick Smythe Series (Crime)

1. The Disappearance of Russell Hadleigh
2. The Graves of Calgary Bay
3. The Fairy Pools Gathering

Austerley & Kirkgordon Series (Fantasy)

1. Crescendo!
2. The Darkness at Dillingham
3. Dagon's Revenge
4. Ship of Doom

Supernatural and Elder Threat Assessment Agency (SETAA) Series (Fantasy)

1. Scarlett O'Meara: Beastmaster

Island Adventures Series (Cosy Fantasy Adventure)

1. Surface Tensions

Dark Wen Series (Horror Fantasy)

1. The Blasphemous Welcome
2. The Demon's Chalice

Chapter 01

We're going to be late.'

Macleod stepped out of the car and saw his partner, Jane, standing at the door. She was tapping the small watch she wore.

'We won't be late. The taxi's not even here yet.'

'No, but you need to get changed.'

'I'll just go like this.'

'No, you won't,' said Jane. 'Those are work clothes. I mean, look at them. Yes, they say serious. Yes, they say I'm a professional; I know what I'm doing. They do not say I'm on a night out with the woman who's made my life a dream.'

'How do the clothes I'm wearing even come into that?' asked Macleod, baffled. But Jane had already run down the driveway and was hauling him inside.

'This retirement is going to change you. You're going to be different. You will not slink around in what you used to wear at work. I get the professionalism. I get the fact that you have to look the part there. Well, get the idea that you have to look the part with me.'

'What do you want me to change into?'

'Well, you're not wearing a tie for a start. See, when we're done, see, when you're done with work, that's it; there are no more ties.'

'But what am I going to wear with the shirts?'

'You're going to get some decent shirts. You're going to get some shirts that are not just white. Shirts that are not completely plain.'

'I take it you've got clothes laid out for me,' said Macleod as he felt himself dragged up the stairs.

'Do you think I would trust you to choose something for a night like this?'

Arriving at the bedroom, Macleod saw the polo shirt. It had been expensive. One that Jane had got him at Christmas that he was yet to really wear. He also saw the trousers. They weren't dark; they were lighter than his normal ones. And then there were the brown shoes. Apparently, it all matched, though he had no idea if it did.

'Change, now. And then you can get that hair brushed.'

Macleod nodded and undressed, aware that Jane was standing watching him.

'No time for that,' said Macleod. 'We've got to get out.'

Jane was tapping her foot, a very serious expression on her face. But then she burst out laughing.

'That's probably why I'm still with you. You know that. You can be funny on occasion.'

He smiled back. He brought that out in her, although he thought he was doing it increasingly at work now, too. Brief moments. Just times when he'd maybe crack the odd joke. Not that he had never had a sense of humour. It was just that he kept it inside. Standing over a dead body, it wasn't easy to make a good quip. Or at least one that he felt would be appropriate. There was respect surrounding the dead. Not one that was always exercised by some of the younger colleagues, but one that he certainly felt should be there. After all, these were people who had passed on. But tonight was different.

He had bought the tickets for Jane well in advance, knowing how she liked Angus Morton, Scotland's darling. The man was older than Macleod, which was why Macleod was taking her, because he didn't feel threatened. However, he was also going to a play in which Angus Morton, Scotland's finest actor of a certain age, was playing a detective. He had suffered worrying thoughts about that. Did he really want to be in the audience?

Ten years ago, not a problem. But now, now that his face had been on the TV so much, he wasn't so sure. Still, Jane had wanted to go, and they needed to do things together. With work, it was always so difficult to find the time, and he'd have to get used to this idea. Every day would have to be an adventure. Every day would have to be something. He wouldn't go into retirement and just sit down. He owed it to her. Jane wanted to travel. Jane wanted to go out and take on the world. And, well, why not, Macleod had thought. Why not?

While he wasn't one for the theatre, Jane loved it, and this was right up her alley. She enjoyed all those crime whodunits on TV, unlike Macleod, who just sat there pointing out the things that were wrong. She told him to shut up. It was just entertainment. And yes, it was just entertainment.

He wondered if people wrote books about his actual working life, would they be interested in him? There were lots of people interested in true crime, and he thought them to be slightly morbid. He had a professional interest in why killers did what they did. There was an interest born of bringing them to justice, in preventing other murders, not in a fascination with the dead and how they died.

'That's the taxi,' said Jane.

As Macleod did up his belt, he pulled out his comb. He went to the bedroom mirror, gave it a quick brush, but in truth, there wasn't much he could do with his hair these days. It just did what it did. He grabbed the jacket that was lying on the bed, one he never really wore. It wasn't a long coat as he liked in work, or a suit jacket. She'd called it a sports jacket, though he didn't see himself doing any sport in it.

As he came down the stairs, Jane looked up from the bottom. 'Now, that's better,' she said. 'There's somebody I can have on my arm as my man.'

And then he stopped. She looked stunning. Radiant. *That's the thing*, he thought. *The older we get, it's the radiance that shines through. I remember being a younger man, and it was the physical attributes. It was skin, the curves. Now, it's the effervescence that came off Jane. Is that the right word? It sounds a bit clinical. She's beautiful, though.* He walked down the stairs, and she grabbed his arm, but he held her.

'The taxi's waiting, come on!'

'Wait,' he said. And she turned, face almost like thunder. 'You look amazing,' said Macleod. A smile broke out across her face, and she gave him a kiss on the cheek.

'Smooth talker,' she said, 'you're going to have to work harder than that for this girl.' She took his hand and pulled him towards the door.

'Wait,' he said. 'Wallet!'

Several minutes later, they were in the back of the taxi heading towards Inverness. He could have sworn there was more traffic than usual on the road for this time of night. Maybe that wasn't surprising. There'd been such a buzz about this production. Here on the opening night, at least it's opening night in Inverness, there was a palpable surge of excitement.

The Ness Theatre, near the River Ness islands, was a reasonable size. You could fit several thousand in to watch a show. And this show had been sold out for two weeks solid, such was the pulling attraction of Angus Morton. Apparently, Sandra Brown was also in it, but Macleod didn't know who that was. And the young and exciting Helen Love.

'It's a Frances Jollye production. She's directing,' said Jane. She was almost bouncing up and down in the seat as they were driven in, making Macleod smile. He'd been slightly later back than he'd said because he was dropping Hope back home. She'd been in for the first couple of days this last month of handover, and then Macleod would be away, off on holiday.

He had dropped her back home because John had taken her car that morning, and it was a good excuse to see the little one. It had been a close call for them on St. Kilda. One he hadn't appreciated, but they'd come through it, Hope and John. Macleod had no qualms about handing over to Hope, about leaving the rest with her. She was good at what she did; she'd learnt well. Hope had taught him some things too. She was ready to take the lead.

And he? He was ready for this, the adventure beside him. He'd got to know Jane, but it was always with a sense of being tied down. Always with a sense that they couldn't be themselves. Not fully. The job was always there. And while that job was a big part of him, it wasn't fully him. He was more than a detective. She'd said that.

As they entered the theatre, Jane directed Macleod to buy a programme and to get them some drinks. Jane had a glass of wine, and Macleod, never one for alcohol, got himself a coke. They took their seats, right in the stalls, about six rows back.

Apparently, this was the prime position to watch. You weren't so low that you looked up to the stage. Instead, you were looking directly at it. At least, that's what someone had told him. And that's why he'd bought these tickets. Of course, Jane was delighted with them, and as they handed their tickets in and went through to their seats, he was impressed by the theatre.

The circle up behind him, little boxes at the side. It was a cultural criss-cross this theatre, half modern, half not. And it was Inverness's theatre.

The show had been running, according to Jane, for the best part of six months. It had taken over two months in Edinburgh, a month in Glasgow. It had even gone to London originally. A tale of a detective finding a body, trying to expose who had done what. Macleod wasn't looking forward to that side of it. But as the curtain went up, and the music came on, Macleod settled back. It was an evening at the theatre, a time to relax, a time to be with Jane. He reached over and grabbed her hand. She leant in and kissed the side of his cheek.

'Thank you,' she said. 'Now shut up and don't tell me about any inconsistencies in the plot.'

He managed not to laugh at that and settled in for the show.

In truth, the show was quite good. The acting was excellent, he thought. Although he was quite surprised by the lack of people on stage. There seemed to be maybe five?

Angus Morton commanded the stage. With slick black-grey hair and despite a body that looked like it had seen its fair days of excess booze and maybe women, he delivered a stunning performance opposite a slightly younger woman. Younger than Macleod, by the looks of it. Sandra Brown played a stunning, red-headed, femme fatale alongside a much younger woman. Presumably Helen Love, if the programme was to be believed.

There were two other men, both fairly young, and one of them was playing several parts. By the time they got to the last scene, Macleod was almost enjoying himself. Sure, the way they'd handled the investigation, how they stomped around and suddenly came up with solutions to this and that, he didn't believe it. And there was a slight character inconsistency at times, not because of the actor, Macleod thought, but because of the plot. He restrained himself, though, and said nothing to Jane.

But now they were at the climax, the all-encompassing last scene. Macleod watched as the detective, played by Angus Morton, strolled about the stage with all the other characters on it, explaining what was happening. As he came to a conclusion, which Macleod wasn't wholly convinced of, he stood looking over at the young actress. Her character was apparently the guilty party, and she looked pretty angry about it.

Macleod watched as she drew a pistol, all the actors on stage suddenly freezing. There were dramatic last moments as Angus Morton's character slowly edged towards her. Then he stood in one final, last, desperate plea to her to put the gun down while it was pointed at him. And then there was a bang.

No, there wasn't, thought Macleod.

Angus Morton was lifted off his feet. He went backwards to the ground, and there was an audible gasp from the audience. But it wasn't one of horror. It was one of delight. One of appreciation for an incredibly well-worked act on stage. Except it wasn't. *That gunshot,* thought Macleod, *was real.*

He stood up, knowing he was right, knowing it when he

saw the faces of the actors. There was a scream from one, and Macleod was barging down the length of his row.

'Out of the way! Out of the way!'

By the time he got to the end of the row and started running for the stage, he could hear screams and shouts beginning amongst the audience. And then there was another voice.

'Stay calm! Sit down! Bloody well sit down!' A tartan shawl was flying towards the stage.

Macleod was able to mount the steps at the side and was on the stage in maybe just more than a minute. The actors had come over and knelt beside Angus Morton. The scene was disgusting. Half of his brain seemed to be across the stage. His head had partially exploded as the bullet must have flown out the back, taking some of the matter with it. Otherwise, the dead man was fairly intact, and Macleod shouted at the actors to stand back.

He raced, however, towards the young actress who had held the gun. Macleod grabbed it from her. He cracked it open. It was a fake. It wasn't real, just an outer shell. On the other side of the stage, looking back at him, he saw Clarissa, the tartan shawl wrapped around her.

He pointed to the back of the stage. 'In there! In there! Seal everywhere off! Seal everything!'

'What the hell are you doing?' said one of the women on stage. 'Who are you?'

'DCI Seoras Macleod. Calm down. Everyone, just calm down. Step away from the body.'

Macleod picked up his phone, calling the station. He asked for assistance, advising they would need an ambulance and lots of police to help. Meanwhile, the audience had their phones out; they were taking pictures of the stage. He waved his arms, telling them all to move back. Clarissa came running back through.

'I haven't seen anyone. They're not back here. Whoever it is, is not back there.'

'Get outside,' said Macleod. 'Everyone stays in. Everyone stays in the building. I'll keep them off the stage. You keep them in the building until the others arrive. I've called for backup.'

She looked anxiously at him because, like him, she knew it was a thankless task. People would surge out. People would want to leave such a horrific scene. But Macleod knew there was no one else better to be outside.

He looked around him, scanned the faces of those on the stage and those out in the audience. He then looked down at Angus Morton. The eyes were open. A single gunshot into the head. The hole at the front was neat. And then he heard a voice.

'Seoras, can I help?' He looked up and saw Jane looking down.

'Go to the edge of the stage. Nobody else up here. Keep them all down there. Okay?'

He turned to the cast who were still on the stage. 'Over there,' he said, pointing to the far end of the stage. 'Stand there together.'

Everywhere he looked, he saw cameras, pictures being taken. Scotland's leading actor, Scotland's beloved treasure, Angus Morton, was lying here dead on stage. There couldn't be a bigger case; there couldn't be a more prominent murder. He realised his evening had taken a turn very much for the worse.

Chapter 02

The red-haired ponytail was obvious as soon as she stepped out of the car, and Macleod almost gave a sigh of relief. The team was coming now. They'd be here, and he could get on with trying to really work out what had happened. In the aftermath, it had been firefighting.

Clarissa had done a terrific job trying to keep everyone inside the building, making sure no one got out or got in. She'd physically stopped certain members of the press. And when the initial set of police cars had arrived, she'd deployed them in a ring around the theatre.

By the time Hope had arrived, there was some degree of order. Macleod was thankful for this. He'd been asked a hundred times already who had killed Angus Morton. While as a police officer you never said 'I don't know' and simply 'Enquiries are beginning', he hadn't a clue what had gone on.

Hope pushed her way through the scrum of reporters, her six feet height allowing her to stride through. She gave a brief grin as she approached Macleod.

'What, you just couldn't get enough of me at work?'

'Don't,' said Macleod. He shook his head and then turned away, realising the press were there. When she got alongside him and followed him inside the theatre, he said, 'This is going to be big, huge.'

'Who's dead?' asked Hope.

'You didn't hear?' he said. 'It's Angus Morton.'

'The Angus Morton,' said Hope. 'No, you're having me on.'

'Shot dead, on stage, in front of me, in front of Clarissa, and in front of the entire audience.'

'Clarissa?'

'She's been terrific. She's kept everything going, ringed off the area. And we're hopefully going to get statements from people. Names, numbers, all the rest of it. I've put a request in for every bit of overtime Uniform can throw our way. I take it Ross and the rest are on their way.'

'I'm surprised they're not here already,' said Hope. 'Susan, Perry, all coming in. Do you want any of the others?'

'No, when Uniform are all here, we'll have enough. There's no need to bring in Emmett or Sabine, or Patterson.'

'Very good. You want me to stay out here?' asked Hope.

'No, come with me. At the moment, I've got one of the sergeants holding the line. He'll be fine until Ross gets here.'

Macleod walked in through the entrance and saw where he'd bought a drink earlier on.

'It was all perfectly normal. Came in, we got our drinks, showed the tickets, we went through to the stage.'

He went up the stairs that led to the stalls, and from there walked Hope inside the theatre. Most of the audience were now being held in corridors just outside the main theatre. Luckily, it wasn't a wet night, and Macleod didn't fancy the idea of processing all these people so quickly. The local sergeant said there were a few buildings nearby they'd get opened and start taking people through but Macleod was more interested in the scene inside.

He walked up the stairs along with Hope.

'I was there,' he said, pointing to the seats in the stalls.

'Nice seats.'

'They were in the last scene, Angus Morton standing mid-stage, a young lady across from him. She raises a gun in the act and shoots him, but it's not a real gun. Not sure where the gun is now, but I checked it. It can't fire anything, not sure it even makes a noise. But it wasn't the sound of a blank being fired we heard. It was a proper gunshot, but most of the audience didn't realize,' said Macleod.

'Got onto the stage. Clarissa had realised, and she was on the stage too. She ran around the outside, but she saw nobody leave the building. She reckoned she was quick enough that anybody fleeing would have been seen, and then she maintained a patrol around the outside until the first Uniforms arrived.'

'So our killer's still in the building.'

'Can't say that,' said Macleod. 'In truth, by the time we got on the stage, they could have gone. There's apparently CCTV, but it's at the front. If somebody came in during the play we might not see them. There's none around the back which is what we really needed.'

Macleod walked over and bent down beside the body.

'Shot in the head,' said Hope, looking down beside him.

'I'm hoping Jona's going to do better than that,' said Macleod.

'Looking at where he's landed, it's coming from over there somewhere.'

'That's the line,' said Macleod. 'That's what I thought. But in that general area, the young actress who shot the false gun is directly in line. Some of the back of his head came away.

People on the stage thought it was just a clever theatrical show.'

'The bullets come out the back, so it must be . . .'

Macleod turned and pointed up to one of the boxes. 'It's at the bottom of that box. You can see the hole.'

'That's good. Forensics should be able to find that. Have you seen anything in the wings? A gun?'

'No,' said Macleod. He was about to walk over to the rear of the stage when he heard a shout.

'Do you mind getting away from my crime scene?' said a voice. Macleod turned and saw the young Asian woman, who was the forensic lead at the station.

'Tell me you're not padding all the way over and around there.'

'I've been all the way over and around here already just after it happened,' said Macleod.

'You were here?'

'Yes,' said Macleod, 'I was here.'

'You all right?' asked Jona.

'It's not my first dead body.'

'No, but you saw him getting shot. I thought we asked that these days.'

'Where's Jane?' asked Hope.

Macleod looked around him suddenly. He'd gone into work mode. He'd gone into work mode, got on the stage. She'd come up. He told her to guard the stage. Then she'd gone. She'd gone somewhere.

'I don't know,' said Macleod. 'I'm in work mode. I'm in . . .'

'You can find her if you want,' said Jona. 'I'm sure Hope can take me through this.'

'I will do,' said Macleod, 'but probably better if I stay and give you the briefing. I was here.'

He ran Jona through what had happened before leaving with Hope out into the foyer. Ross was there at a table, a number of uniformed officers around him.

'Just getting briefed, sir,' said Ross. 'Thought we needed to maintain the line.'

'You'd better maintain it,' said a voice from the side. A tartan shawl emerged, and Ross stared at Clarissa. 'I've kept it for you, Als. Sorted it out for you. Not a problem. Make sure it's tight. The press will be all over this one.'

'When you're done,' said Macleod to Ross, 'I need to see everybody for just a minute or two.'

Ross nodded. Macleod saw Hope chasing down Perry and Susan. It was then that Macleod saw Jane sitting on a chair just inside the foyer. He left the team to see to her.

'Are you okay?' he asked. He put his arms on her shoulders, scanning her face. 'I'm sorry, I just went into work mode. I just . . .'

'I think I'm okay,' she said. 'I take it he's . . .'

'He's dead,' said Macleod. 'Dead straight away. Took a bullet through the . . .'

'I don't need to know the details,' said Jane. 'I'm not asking for a breakdown.'

'Course not,' said Macleod. 'Sorry, I just go into mode. This is what I do. Not for long though.' She smiled at him. 'And you did great,' he said. 'You helped. You were . . .'

'It seemed better than doing nothing. Seemed better than just sitting there and you had no one. You just had Clarissa. You just . . .'

'It's going to be a long night,' said Macleod. 'You want me to get someone to take you home? Get someone to sit with you. You've just seen someone shot. Many people have.'

'I'll be fine,' said Jane.

He observed her carefully. She wasn't herself. There were definitely tremors there.

'You're going to stay here for a moment.' He picked up his mobile phone and called a colleague.

'This is Emmett. Do you need help? I've seen the news.'

'I need help, Emmett, but it's of a personal nature. Jane and I were at the theatre when it happened. She's seen what happened. Can you come over with Sabine, take Jane home, and sit with her till I get back?'

'Of course,' said Emmett, 'of course we can. Is she in shock?'

'I don't think so, but keep an eye on her. Your call, if you think she needs to see a doctor or anyone for shock, call it and do it. It'll be busy tonight, though. I think there could be quite a few people in shock. Packed theatre. They all saw him getting shot.'

'I'll be over in about a half hour at the most.'

'Thank you, Emmett.'

'You don't need us beyond that?' he asked.

'We should have enough. We've got plenty of Uniform coming in. I'd rather you not come in and then I can use you later if I need to give the others a break.'

'Of course,' said Emmett. 'Be there in half an hour.'

Macleod held Jane's hand for a moment, explained what was happening. When she went to protest, he simply put his finger up to her lips. 'This is my world. I'm doing what's right,' he said. 'You go along with it on this one. There are no arguments. There's no disagreement. No changing Seoras's mind,' he said. 'This is the DCI talking, okay?'

She nodded, and he kissed her forehead. He turned and saw that Hope had gathered his team together.

'Right. Jona's doing her work,' said Macleod. 'So we keep that area clear, let her get on with it. Clarissa, help the sergeant out. He's maintaining the cordon here, just for tonight. Those press rats will be devious; they'll be desperate for a photo of Morton, desperate for any coverage they can get.'

'I'll sort them,' she said. 'You want me to take care of Jane too?'

'Emmett's coming with Sabine. Don't worry about Jane; they'll look after her. I need you to do a job for me.'

'I'll get Frank to go to Jane tonight; it'll give her something to do. Make a bed up for him,' said Clarissa. 'I take it I'll be here most of the night.'

'If you would,' said Macleod. He then turned to Perry and Susan. 'We're going to need interviews. The actors and the stagehands particularly—that'll be me, and Hope here. We're going to need to get interviews of everybody who was in the theatre, see if anybody saw anything, get statements. I want you to round up some Uniform and do that. Perry, Susan, and Ross, stay over the top, making sure everything happens, make sure Jona is happy.

'Obviously, we're all at home here, so we don't need to do anything for digs, but we're going to need to work out of an incident room. Make sure that's set up either in the station or if we need a local one, here,' Macleod said to Ross. 'Hope and I are going to run over the top of this. That's what we'll need from the rest of you, okay? Ross, when you get a chance, get into the background of all these actors, of the production, everything. Was there a director here tonight?'

'I believe there was,' said Perry. 'She's with the actors and the actresses at the moment. We've got them separate, I believe, according to the sergeant.'

'That's correct,' said Ross. 'They're separate and being held apart. The audience are in different parts of the building at the moment. Apparently, we've got another nearby building, so we're going to lead them through, away from the press. We'll do our processing in there, statements and the like, try to clear them before morning. Get everybody home as soon as we can.'

'Good,' said Macleod. 'Do that. It's what you're good at, Ross. Perry, Susan, you're with him. And then in the morning we'll hopefully have some idea of what happened. The CCTV needs to be picked up as well.'

'Already on it,' said Ross. Macleod nodded and let his team disappear, except for Hope, who he drew to one side.

'This one is going to be in the public eye. Angus Morton, much as I'm not into the theatre or anything like that, I'm well aware of what a celebrity he was. Every bit of his life's going to be picked out. There's going to be demands to find the killer, and if we don't, it's going to get worse. There's going to be all sorts of theories. We've got a public who saw the murder, and they're going to give lots and lots of descriptions once they clear Ross and his interview team. This is going to be a media circus like we have not seen before.'

'It's all right,' said Hope. 'I can handle it.'

'I know you can handle it, but I'm going to take this one.'

'You're done,' said Hope. 'You're about to go on your holiday. Done! You don't need to take it. You can assist me; be here with me. Give me your ideas. It's not a problem. I'm good. I'm ready to roll.'

'It's not that,' said Macleod.

'Then what?' she asked, clearly miffed.

'I have no qualms about your taking on this case. I have no doubt that you could get to the bottom of it, eventually. But whoever leads this case will be hauled through it. Whoever is in charge of it will be decried for not doing this, not doing that. Even if they get to the bottom of it, there'll be something. There will be something that will sit with them for the rest of their career. You have, so far, had an exemplary career. But it's only just beginning. I've had mine and I couldn't care less what they slap on me now. I'm gone. And if you take it and you don't find a killer, it'll be Macleod would have solved that. Macleod would have solved this. Macleod would have done that. Hope, I'm going to take this one.'

'You don't need to protect me.'

'I do,' said Macleod. 'I really do. This isn't me being sentimental. This is me making sure. You'll get the gravitas and authority in the years to come that you deserve and I won't let you get derailed by some media circus over a trumped-up actor.'

She hung her head for a moment, and he put his hand on her shoulder. 'Hope, let me take it. One last time, you and me, but like the old days; this is my last case. This is it. I'm not doing it out of sentiment. I'm doing it to protect you, and to take away any flak that comes from it. And there will be flak. There will be stuff that will stick. Let the old man do that for you.'

She nodded. 'Okay,' she said. 'Okay, it's your call, anyway. I understand but I don't agree with it.'

'I never wanted somebody with me who agreed with me. Come on then,' he said. 'We've got a busy night.'

Chapter 03

'Seriously? They were seriously putting on a production with just these people? Five actors?' asked Hope.

'There were only the five,' said Macleod. 'One of them seemed to play a lot of different parts. One of the younger ones, but yes, that was it.'

Macleod was in an office on the upper floors of the theatre, awaiting the house manager and the overall director of the theatre. They came in together, an older woman and a middle-aged man.

'Good evening, Inspector. Terrible. It's just terrible,' said the woman. 'My name's Sarah Coghill.' She was blonde-haired in her late sixties, and looked tremendously shaken up. Beside her was a small man, with balding hair and glasses. 'This is Martin Brough,' she said. 'Martin basically runs the place.'

'I believe there are only five actors and a director with this show,' said Macleod.

'That's right,' said Martin. 'In truth, those of us here at Ness Theatre, we've had very little to do with it. We've basically handed over the stage. They've got five actors, there's a director, and their main stage crew only comprises three people.'

'Where's the musicians?' asked Macleod.

'Oh, there are no musicians,' said Martin.

'There was music at the start. There was music during the interval.'

'It's recorded. It's too expensive to bring musicians too when it's not a musical. In fact, I don't know the ins and outs of the budget that the production was running, because you understand that it's their production. We were just providing the shell. We also provide staff to do the front of house, the tickets and that, and to do the stewarding. However, the actual production and the lights and all that are done by them. Yes, they use some of our gear, but it's being done by them.'

'Right,' said Macleod. 'So, all of your people were . . .'

'. . .at the front of house. So, they're in the theatre hall itself, or in the corridors on the public side, or in the circle or the stalls. Before the show, in the entrance foyer, manning the reception, manning the drinks, the bars and the food stalls. Selling programmes.'

'Anyone round the back?'

'No, actually. The director, Frances Jollye, was very specific about that. They don't like anyone at the back. In fact, we haven't been round the back in . . . oh, since the cleaners were in. No one else has since they started setting up and rehearsing. They don't like people about. I think that might be Angus Morton who stipulated that, God rest his soul.'

'Okay,' said Macleod, 'so I saw this show, but my colleague here, DI McGrath, didn't. Can we run through everyone who was backstage or who was in the production?'

'Okay,' said Martin. 'Angus Morton, obviously, who's died. He was playing DCI McNeil in the production. Playing Scarlet Mist was Sandra Brown, and then you had Alistair Pies. He was Hans Imman. Rupert Warrello played different people, but Kyle Vasquez was his main character. And then Helen Love was playing Judy Swift.'

'I recognise Angus Morton,' said Hope, 'but I'm not particularly a theatre person. The rest of them—are they famous?'

'Well, Sandra Brown, you would have known by appearance at least; she's appeared in a lot of different productions. Though she's not a household name, she's certainly a household face. The other three, probably not. Helen Love maybe. Helen Love did a lot of work as a child actress and has come through the ranks. So, she's fairly well-known. Though probably most people would remember her being younger in other productions. So, they might not tally her face-to-face straight away.'

'And the director—what about her?' asked Hope.

'Frances Jollye. She's well known for getting things done on a tight budget. Angus Morton would have taken most of the budget for this production. Frances is used to working on low-scale, very high-quality productions. She's quite a talent.'

'And who else does she have with her then?'

'Dieter Hans was the main stage crew leader. He would probably have been up on the desk doing the lights and the sound. They had Julie Flipp and Peter Brush, two younger crew. They would have been running around doing any of the scenery changes, any of the costume help. Julie was quite good with the costumes. I think she covers that side of it.'

'Full list of those please, if you would, Martin. And hand them to my sergeant, Ross,' said Macleod. 'I think I'm going to talk to the actors initially.' He turned to Hope. 'That could take quite a while. I want to interview them singly.'

'Shall I get Perry and Susan to cover off the stage crew then?'

'Yes, get them to do an initial interview with them. See what they knew. Find out where they were when he was shot.' He turned back to the Ness Theatre staff.

'Well, thank you, Martin and Sarah. Once your people have made a statement to our uniformed colleagues, they'll be cleared to go. We won't look to get too much from them. What I would ask, though, is that you make sure that you talk to them. Any of them inside will have seen Angus Morton being shot. They may get an adverse reaction to that. I would take excellent care of your staff at this time.'

'Of course,' said Sarah. 'I'll organise that.'

'You and I,' said Macleod to Hope, 'need to speak to someone first. Let's talk to Helen Love first. She was holding the gun that didn't kill him.'

Hope picked up her phone and called Ross, and then turned to Macleod, indicating she should follow her.

He descended the stairs and was suddenly in the back rooms of the theatre. Corridors that went here and there, and Macleod truly didn't know where he was. Hope seemed to be more aware. Then Macleod stopped, seeing Clarissa scrambling across a corridor.

The tartan shawl was flying, and he picked up his pace to follow her. As he reached the corner she'd disappeared around, he saw her with her hands on the back of a man's neck.

'Where are you going?' she said. 'Out! Out! I don't want to see your face on the press line. I don't want to see your face anywhere near here. You were told not to break the police line. You come across again, I'll arrest you. Understand?'

Macleod turned and began following Hope again, almost chuckling to himself. His Rottweiler was on patrol, but he wouldn't say that to her. That was the thing about Clarissa though, she knew all the old tactics; she knew how devious people could be. She trusted no one, not really, not truly, and she could scare people without making a big deal of it. The last thing you needed to do was to upset the press by arresting them all, but they needed to be clear of the scene. She knew the line to walk, and she strode it well.

Hope led Macleod to a dressing room, and when he knocked on the door, it was opened up by a paramedic. Entering the room, he asked the paramedic how his patient was and if they could have a moment with the woman.

'Miss Love's okay. She's in shock. We've given her a cup of tea. She needs nothing medically at the moment, but as she's just seen something horrible, I don't think she should be left alone. On the other hand, she's not really needing medical attention.'

'Thank you,' said Macleod. 'We'll make sure somebody's with her when we leave. We'll let you get back to your work.'

The paramedic left, and Macleod turned to Helen Love. 'I'm DCI Macleod. This is DI McGrath. We just want to ask you some questions.'

'You're him,' said Helen. 'You're the man who came on the stage.'

'Yes,' he said. 'Obviously, you've had a bit of a shock. The gun you were holding, it's not responsible. It doesn't have the capacity to fire anything. I knew that once I took it off you.'

'I knew that too,' said Helen. 'Obviously, it's a prop, but I was there, and that was the timing. That's when I was meant to fire, and the gun makes a sound, but not that sound.'

'No, it doesn't make that sort of sound if it's a fake,' said Macleod.

'And then he got lifted off his feet. I saw the, oh God,' she blurted, 'the bits that came out the back. That wasn't meant to happen. The blood, that wasn't—'

'It's okay,' said Macleod. 'It's a horrible sight, but I need to ask you some questions. Did you know Angus Morton well?'

The woman looked incredulously at Macleod. 'Everyone knows Angus Morton. Angus Morton is, well, he's been such an actor for years. It's tragic. It's a tragic loss. I've wanted to be in a play with Angus since I was a young girl. My older sister, she got a part in the play with him. And—'

'When was that?' asked Hope.

'Several years ago, now. It wasn't a big part, but she was on stage with him. She loved it too. Said he was terrific, and was very taken with him.'

'And that's what made you want to be on stage with him too?' asked Macleod.

'Not just that. I mean, he's such an actor, and after my sister died last year, getting to do this, getting to be up here, getting to, oh, I was so happy. We were on tour, months, months of learning from the man, months of getting together.'

'You were with the show down in London.'

'No, no, no. No, they did the show down in London, and most of the actors changed. I've been with them since we took over in Glasgow, taking it out to the regions.'

'That's quite popular these days, isn't it?' said Hope. 'They tour after an initial run down in London or somewhere big.'

'It's quite something, because you get so much access to them. They're not disappearing off to their homes or hotels in London. Instead, you get more of a camaraderie,' said Helen.

'How did your sister die,' asked Macleod, 'if you don't mind me asking?'

The woman clearly did and burst into tears. They waited for

her to settle again. Macleod looked around the room. It was fairly standard. There wasn't an enormous bunch of flowers or anything like is often portrayed in theatre dressing rooms. Instead, the room was fairly bare, except for some bags, which presumably contained Miss Love's clothing.

'My sister took her own life last year. She struggled for years with drink and drugs. And I'm afraid that's really come back to me. The whole link between her and him and . . . I just . . . Well . . .' She began to cry again. Macleod looked over at Hope, who turned to Helen.

'I appreciate this is difficult, but . . . your sister was an actress, you said. And then suffered with drugs and drinking?'

'It's the pressures. People don't get how pressured it is up here. And you've got to make things happen, haven't you? And when you're young, when you're this age, it's not the same as it is for Sandra.'

'You mean Sandra Brown, the actress playing Scarlet Mist?'

'Yes. Sandra's terrific. She's a great actress. Learned so much from her,' said Helen. 'But it's not the same for her. Nobody looks at her and thinks, well, they look at her acting, don't they? They don't always look at me like that. Instead they look at, well, you know.'

'They look at you like you're an object,' said Hope. 'I get it. It can happen when you're on TV with the police as well.'

'Well, when Sandra's in the paper,' said Helen, 'they don't comment on whether Sandra's boobs are still looking great. Sometimes I think all they want to know about in the paper is how my boobs are.'

Macleod left Hope to ask the next question, unsure of quite how to push what he wanted to know.

'Do you think that's why you were brought into the production?' asked Hope.

'I can act,' said Helen, defensively.

'I wasn't suggesting you couldn't,' said Hope, 'but I'm a detective. While I can solve crimes as well as the best of them, they still want me to be doing the press interviews rather than my colleague here.'

Well, that is true, thought Macleod.

'It's the same for all young women,' said Helen. 'Look at your figure. Does your bum get bigger? Did this happen? You know? And then you get the nastier papers, wanting to know if you're playing a part without any clothes on. Even if you do it for good reasons and the role demands it, they still want to know all about it. That they still treat it like it's some sort of sexual act.'

'Would you say you were placed here as the glamour in this production?' asked Hope.

'I'm nineteen. Sandra's Forty-seven. The rest are men. I'm certainly the female glamour bit, aren't I?'

'And your director, Frances, she would pick you for that reason?'

'Frances doesn't always get to pick who she wants. She has to deal with whomever she is given often. It's to do with finances. I'm not exactly expensive, and Angus would have been very expensive. Sandra would command a fair bit, too. Not on Angus's level. Me, at the moment, I have to pick up whatever jobs I can get my hands on.'

'But you applied for this one.'

'You apply for them all,' said Helen. 'You take what you can get, and you make your money. I'm nineteen, I'm still learning, and not yet established . Not like Sandra. Not like Angus, certainly.'

'Is there anything over the last few months,' asked Macleod, 'that would indicate to you that somebody wanted to kill Angus?'

'Not from within the group,' said Helen. 'You always get a bit of fracas when you're rehearsing and that, but generally, we were pretty good. And Frances keeps everything within our small company. We didn't have any trouble with the theatre people. They got out of our way. I don't know why somebody wanted to kill him. Doesn't really make sense, does it?'

Macleod watched as the woman began crying again. That's when it hit him. He was interviewing people here like he always interviewed people, looking to see what pressure they were under, how they responded. But here he was in a world of actors and actresses. To anything he said, they could act back an appropriate response. How would he know if they were acting, especially if they were any good?

He watched as Helen cried some more. It wasn't worth continuing at the moment, anyway. He'd see what the rest said. Helen, at the end of the day, had been on stage and was firing a gun that couldn't shoot any projectile. And that was the problem. The circumstances put everybody on stage in the clear.

Chapter 04

Macleod and Hope were directed by Ross into another changing room, which had the name Sandra Brown on the outside. This was different from Helen Love's room, as her name did not appear on her dressing room door. Macleod knocked sharply, and a tacit 'Come in' was heard. On opening the door, he could see that Sandra Brown was not alone. The red-haired woman was sitting in a dressing gown, and across from her was a middle-aged man who Macleod recognised as being Hans Inman in the play.

'I'm DCI Seoras Macleod and this is DI Hope McGrath.'

'Ah, the man who ran onto the stage. That explains why you were able to handle it so well. You did handle it well,' said the woman.

'Mr Pies, I take it,' said Macleod to the man.

'Alistair Pies, yes. We were just sitting chatting afterwards, with nowhere else to go. We're kind of kept here.'

'Prisoners,' said Sandra, 'prisoners all tied up, waiting to be interrogated.'

Macleod understood these were actors, but he didn't think the theatrics were really appropriate when one of their number had died.

'Is this the first time either of you has been involved with a death on stage?'

'No,' said Sandra. 'The old fart, what did you call him? Michael. Michael Dermont. He died. A heart attack. Nothing so dramatic as tonight. But he died of a heart attack right there on stage in front of us. We were up and running the show the next night. In saying that, I don't know with this one.'

'Have you been with the production since the start?' asked Hope.

'Yes,' said Sandra. 'They wanted a big name, obviously, down in London. So, Angus was the big name. But they also needed some sort of backup. If you don't put around the big names, people who are decent and know who can handle the pressure of performing with a name, they get nervous. I can handle the role. I'm what they call a journey woman. That's how they say it?'

'What does that mean?' asked Macleod.

'It means that I can act—I can act well—but I've never been one to grab all the limelight and be held up as a national treasure, despite all the nonsense that I get up to.'

Macleod stared for a moment. 'You're not referring to yourself as getting up to nonsense, are you?'

'No. I'm referring to Angus.'

'Can I just say, you're taking it very well, his death.'

'Well, darling,' said Sandra, and she reached over to grab a glass of whisky that was beside her chair. 'Oh, sorry, did you want any? I take it you don't do that, do you, when you're working?'

Macleod waved a 'no' with his hand. Meanwhile, Alistair stood up, grabbed the bottle that was on the side, and charged

Sandra's glass again, despite the fact it was still less than half empty. He charged his own.

'To the old bugger,' said Sandra, knocking back some of the whisky.

'You were saying he wasn't pristine,' said Macleod. 'I'm not sure that's an image shared by the press.'

'What does the press know? Press knows what we feed them. The press knows what it is told to say. The press is there to promote things, not to report facts, not to find out the truth. You're there to find out the truth,' said Sandra. 'That's true, isn't it? That's right—you're there to get to the bottom of things.'

'Well, we hope so,' said McGrath.

'The press—well, it's not just the press; it's the whole theatre showbiz—is there to support the people who invest the money. You see, Angus was a bit of a bad boy, really.'

'A bad boy?' said Hope.

'Oh yes, and the things of the past are bound to catch up with you at some time. You can paper over the cracks but the cracks come out. In any house, the cracks are still there and the cracks will make themselves known over time to a point where you can't then patch the cracks. They're too big. And then the whole house falls down, doesn't it?'

'True, darling,' said Alistair. 'That's absolutely true.'

'What cracks?' asked Macleod.

'Oh, so many.'

'What cracks?' asked Macleod. 'Specifically. Specifically, what cracks? What are you referring to? Because at the moment, you sound like the press.'

Sandra shot a look at him. 'Never associate me with that lot. They jump into bed with a story. I'm a class actress, okay? I've trod the boards for years, and I've kept my nose clean.

Don't think I haven't had my fun. We've had fun, haven't we, Alistair? Oh, yes. Shag, but don't tell, you know? Nothing with the younger ones. Not, well, not too young anyway. There was that, oh, boy, last time.'

'Boy?' queried Macleod.

'He was twenty-five,' said Alistair. 'They are all boys and girls to us at our age.'

Macleod nodded. 'The thing is,' said Sandra, 'Angus used to gamble, party, drink a lot. He's had affairs; he's had dodgy loans. None of which you'll find anywhere, none of which you'll get to dig up very easily. Always out of money. And in fact, they said the Mafia was into him at one point.'

'The Mafia?' said Macleod. 'Is that the whisky talking?'

Sandra suddenly stood up. She held her hand out in front of Macleod. It was steady as a rock.

'I can hold my drink, love. You're the police. I'm telling you what I know. I'm not making things up. Not trying to be a tell-tale as the press would have it. Someone with slanderous and malicious gossip. I am telling you what is out there and what people have said. Do I have hard facts for it all? Of course not. Because anybody who wants to cover that up has to make sure there won't be any.'

'The man you're describing is not the man that I know. He's a national treasure,' said Hope.

'National treasure,' said Sandra. 'That's the thing, isn't it? When you get to that status, when you become a national treasure'—she waved her hand in front of her as if there was something wrong with the idea—'well, then you can do what you want, can't you? Plenty of national treasures have fallen down.'

'But why would anybody protect them these days?' asked

Hope.

'Why did they protect them in the old days? Too much hanging on them. The man's involved with brands. He's advertised this, that, and whatever. As you said, he's a national treasure. A Scottish national treasure,' said Sandra.

'Damn right,' said Alistair. 'You tell him.' He dropped back another shot of whiskey.

'The thing about national treasures is, you've got to remember, he's opened the Commonwealth Games. He's been seen around the Royals up here. Done shows for them at Balmoral, at Christmas. He has been in every walk of public life. He's endorsed big brands. Big Scottish brands. Then you find out he's not pristine. You find out he's done things and things that are not good. All of these people they're in it; they get tainted with it. That's the thing, isn't it? When it flies, when it hits the fan, it goes everywhere.'

'Poop here, poop there, poop landing on everyone,' said Alistair. He reached over with his glass and Sandra gave hers a chink on his.

'What about on stage?' asked Macleod. 'How did you get on with him? I mean, knowing this, what you've just said, and he's touring with you, how did you get on with him?'

'Fine, he's a consummate professional when he's on the boards. That's the thing, you've got to do what you do well. I'm a consummate professional and didn't like the man. He could be a little dick at times, with how up his own self he was, but we're professionals. The production was good. Frances is a professional. He's on board because he's a professional and he's a great actor. Understand that. He could do that part well.'

'What happens to the play now?' asked Macleod. 'Angus is the big star. Is it going to affect you?'

'Might affect some of the others, but it won't affect me,' said Sandra. 'I have enough standing. I'm in demand. They might not want me to headline, but I'll pick up roles, no problem. Alistair here will survive.'

'Just take a rest up until the next one comes along,' said Alistair, waving a hand nonchalantly.

'Alistair picks up enough work,' said Sandra. 'Same as me. Decent, quality actors like us, we'll always find something. You might not enjoy it. But when you're overlooked for the good stuff because you don't have the notoriety'—she waved her fingers to indicate quotes around notoriety—'then you have to just take what you take and get paid for it. We'll be fine. Pity he's dead, but I'll still get paid for this. I was booked in for a long run. It's in my contract. They're paying me for those. They can try to fight their way out of that one.'

'So,' said Macleod. 'You can't tell me if anyone wanted him dead. But you can tell me he was a bad boy and so probably someone did.'

'If I had proof of something, I'd give it to you. Because it's an absolute pain in the arse. I had the next couple of months sorted. Now, I don't.'

'You two have known each other for long?' asked Macleod, pointing at Sandra and Alistair..

'Just been in the biz. That's all,' said Sandra.

'Don't leave town.'

'Well, I'm in the hotel for the rest of the week. We were here for at least a week. I'm not planning on going anywhere.'

'Good,' said Macleod. 'I may need to speak to you again.'

'You are aware we were on stage though,' said Alistair. 'Neither of us was holding a gun.'

'Yes,' said Macleod. 'On the face of it, it would seem to rule you out.'

'Absolutely,' said Sandra.

'But on the face of it doesn't cut any ice,' said Macleod. 'On the face of it, you told me, Angus is a national treasure, but underneath he isn't. So like I say, on the face of it doesn't rule you out either. Thank you for your time.'

Macleod left the room, followed by Hope, and stepped a couple of doors down where Ross said he'd lined up the next actor. Knocking on the door, he was let in by Rupert Worrello, who seemed to shake a lot.

'Are you okay, Mr Worrello? I'm DCI Macleod. This is DI McGrath.'

'Terrible, isn't it? It's terrible, but, you know, it's a star, isn't it? He's a star. He got shot. J.F. Kennedy got shot, didn't he? John Lennon shot. Lots of stars have been shot in their time, haven't they?'

'Did you know Angus well?' asked Hope.

'Picked up in Glasgow. Not been in the production long. Didn't really talk to me, except when he wanted to pass on notes, wanted to pass on advice. No, I didn't really know him.'

'Do you know of anybody who'd want to kill him?'

'Don't know him,' said Rupert. 'Really don't know him. I mean, he's a national treasure. I know what you know from the press. He's not really, well, he's not always that well-liked by certain actors and actresses, but . . .'

'Why's that?' asked Macleod.

'They say things about him, but I know nothing. I don't actually know anything about him.'

'You're very nervous.'

'Somebody just blew a man's brains out in front of me,' said Rupert.

'But you were on stage. It will not be you, will it?' said Macleod.

The man turned suddenly and grabbed a bottle of vodka in the corner. He didn't pour a glass of it but just uncapped it and started to drink it neat.

'That's not very advisable,' said Hope.

'I want to go back to the hotel,' said Rupert. 'I want to go back to the hotel.'

'Why?'

'Because, well, this was a chance, wasn't it? This was a chance. Who knows me? Who knows Rupert Warrello? And there's me playing Kyle Vasquez and all these other parts. That's how it happens. That's what happens to you, isn't it? You get in a small bit with a big actor and then they learn about you. Then you go to the next bit and the next bit. And now I'm in *The One*. I'm in the play that he died in. It's not what you want. You want to be in the one that was a success, that was a triumph. And you helped with that. Not the one where he got killed.'

The sweat was dripping off Rupert. Macleod wondered. The man drank more from the bottle.

'I'd like you to hold off on that for a bit,' said Macleod.

'Why?' asked Rupert.

'Because we like our questions answered when sober,' said Macleod. 'You said you didn't really know him. What about the rest of the cast? And your director? Your stage crew? Do you know any of them?'

'No,' said Rupert. 'No, I've not been up this part of the world either. I'm only twenty-five. Really, most of the stuff I did was down on the south coast of England. And when I got into more stuff, it's been in London, but really low-level stuff in London. In fact, I've worked in the theatre and backstage for a while. That's all. This is quite a big production for me.'

'What are your intentions at the moment? You're going to stay at the hotel?' asked Hope.

'I have no work to go to,' said Rupert. 'This was my work. This was me for the next few months. I don't know whether the contract means I'm going to get paid or not, so I'm going to stay in the hotel, all right. They're paying for that one. Yes, I'll stay there. But I don't know when they'll pull the plug on that one. At least I get my meals in there.

'It's difficult. Angus, you know, he'd got so much money. Sandra's had a . . . well, if you listen to her, she's got years behind her. She always seems comfortable—the same with Alistair. They're not desperate for the work. They need the work to pay bills, but they're not so desperate needing money for food and a roof over their head. I am. I can't afford for this not to be running. Don't know what's going to happen.' He drank again from the bottle.

'Is there anything you can tell me?' asked Macleod. 'Anything that would indicate that somebody wanted to kill Angus.'

'I told you I know nothing. I just want to go back to the hotel.'

'What are you going to do at the hotel?'

'See that bottle there? There's another two or three of them back at the hotel. I'm just going to drink and wake up sometime tomorrow. It's a bloody nightmare. Bloody nightmare.'

Macleod thanked him for his time, and he walked out to the corridor outside.

'What do you make of him?' asked Macleod.

'Somebody who probably has had his finances cut for the next while. He looks genuinely frightened for his career, and for his immediate future.'

'He does, doesn't he? Quite a contrast to the other two.'

'Helen Love too—she looks well, distraught. And she's not handling it.'

'Let's see our director,' said Macleod. 'See how she's taking it.'

Chapter 05

'Miss Jollye, are you in? Miss Jollye?'

Macleod looked at Hope and then turned the handle on the door, finding the door to be unlocked. He pushed into what looked like an office. On one side was a desk with a woman sitting in a chair behind it.

Her eyes were firmly fixed on the wall, but what struck Macleod was that there was nothing on that wall. Other walls had some posters, images of shows that had been at the theatre. There was also a laptop on top of the desk and a screen, but the woman simply looked off at the wall.

Macleod reckoned she couldn't have been much past thirty-five, if that at all. Her hair was brown with ringlets, and there was a distinctly Roman nose. She didn't wear any make-up, was dressed in a black long-sleeved T-shirt, and at the moment, looked like she'd been staring at Medusa, so little did she move.

'Miss Jollye? Frances Jollye?' asked Macleod.

'Yes,' came the single-word answer.

'I'm Detective Chief Inspector Macleod. This is my colleague, Detective Inspector Hope McGrath.'

'The man who ran onto the stage. Yes?'

'I'd like to have a word,' said Macleod. 'Is it okay to do so?

Are you feeling up to questions?'

'I don't know if I'll feel up to anything ever again. No, not after this. But ask away, Inspector.'

'Am I right in believing you're the director?'

'The director, not quite the producer, almost everything but. I'm a stage manager, too. I'm doing everything basically, if it doesn't involve acting, lights or moving props about. Add some editing of the play as well.'

'That's not normal, is it?' asked Hope.

'It's the way I've worked for a long time. I've worked with tiny groups. Apparently, it's what I do best, or at least it was.'

'Was?' asked Hope.

'In this business, you get known for things. I was known for the Hamlet I did, on a shoestring. That was the first one,' said Frances. 'Triumph, marvel. And yes, they trot those words out, here, there and everywhere, but I was nobody; they didn't have to. But still they did. And another one followed, and another one. Eventually, they saw me as a rising star. Someone who could pull together something out of nothing. Small band of actors and minimal backstage and make a success of it. They saw a low-budget, big-profit production.'

'And now?' asked Macleod.

'Now, well, what will I be known for now? Well, the one where Angus Morton died. Died during my play.'

'But you didn't kill him,' said Macleod, 'at least as far as I know.'

'Like that's going to matter to them. Oh no, you get tainted with things. You get brought down because of it. Why would you want a director everybody's got to talk about in terms of what happened? In terms of Angus's death. No longer a young and vibrant director. No, a tragic director. And tragic director doesn't sell. Tragic actor, actress, yes. Because nobody sees us. Directors are there to get it up and get it on stage. What they rate us on is what they see. Not who we are. What did they see this time? A man shot dead on stage. Not just a man, but a national treasure.'

'Is that what you thought of Angus?' asked Macleod.

'Man was a prick.'

'I'm sorry?' said Macleod.

'I said the man was a prick. First class. Numero uno. Couldn't have been a bigger one.'

'Okay,' said Macleod. 'But you were working with him. Did you ask to work with him?'

'Nobody asks to work with Angus. You get handed Angus. And his name attached to the play was going to be a big break for me. Our reviews were great. Not just about Angus, but about me, too. Able to handle a big star. It was tight bringing him in. He wanted a lot of money. I mean, he's got lots of money. It wouldn't have been that long before he was dead, anyway. What did he need all the money for? But does he come in and give an air of grandiose to those struggling still on their way up? No, of course he doesn't. It's Angus. Like I told you, he was a prick.'

'So, he should have done it for free,' said Hope.

'Not for free. Do nothing for free,' said Frances. 'You do it for free, they expect it for free next time. But you can do it for a fee that's reasonable. A fee that allows others to be taken on board. He was swallowing up massive amounts of the budget. But we were making it, and we were doing it well. And running with a backstage crew of three. Three people. It's hilarious. Hilarious. And he knew that. And he still bitched. He still went on and on during rehearsals. Go there, come here, do this, do that, do this. What about my costume? What about that?'

'This may seem like a stupid question after what you've said, but do you know if anyone would want to kill him?' asked Hope.

Frances laughed. 'Excuse me,' she said. 'Where are my manners? Have a seat.'

Macleod entered the room further and sat down, Hope taking a chair beside him. Frances stood up and sat now on the edge of the desk.

'Sorry for being a little down in the dumps, having been right and royally screwed,' she said, 'but I'll see what I can do for you now.'

'I was asking, do you know of anybody who would want him dead?' reiterated Hope.

'I know plenty of people who would want him dead, but dead in the sense that you think it, not in the sense that you would do it. He thought he was a god. And in fairness to him, when people treat you like one, I guess that's what you can become. Ideally, I wouldn't have worked with him, but it gets your name out there, doesn't it? A name like his. Suddenly, you become a director in the public eye, not just in the art world. Directors initially, their work gets looked at by those who have put on productions and know you can do it. And that's good; it keeps you in work. But with a name like Angus, suddenly you become something. And then you get bigger roles, you get bigger projects to look at. Maybe even one day go on to producing.'

'So, you didn't work well with him?' asked Macleod.

'Oh, I worked well with him. I'm a director. Have to be able to work with anybody. I've worked with complete idiots.

Nice people, but complete idiots. I've worked with some nasty buggers. You also get the ones who, well, are truly not nice people. You see some of them going after the younger actresses, and some of them after the younger boys.'

'Sort of older male actors?' asked Macleod.

'Older female actors, too. Young twenty-somethings are what they want. They think they're God's gift to women, or men if they are that way inclined. Young women looking to advance their way up the ladder. You get it all in this game. And you get nice, decent people. Sandra Brown, for instance. Sharp, understands the business, done well for herself. A superb actress, easy to work with, gets her job done, moves on. Drinks like a fish, but never drunk on set, never drunk, stepping out on that stage. A pro.'

'What about the rest of them?' asked Hope.

'Honestly, Alistair, not much of an actor, but he's competent. He gets there, doesn't cause you too much hassle. Rupert, excitable, but he's got a lot of different roles to do. You need somebody who's pumped and desperate to be doing that stuff, and Helen, well, Helen's here because, well . . .'

'What?' asked Hope.

'Helen's here because she's young and attractive. And the producer, at one point, wanted a young, attractive actress opposite Angus. You bring in the national treasure, and then you bring in someone with a big pair of boobs.'

'What?' blurted Macleod.

'We're not doing Shakespeare here. We're not doing a deep and meaningful play. Selling this play off the back of Angus. And that's why we're now screwed. Helen is a good-enough actress. She's young, with lots to learn in some ways. Looks great. That's all she needs to do. She needs to be the bit of glamour that Angus doesn't have. I have got competent people, Sandra and Alistair, to carry it along with Angus, and I've got a decent stage crew at the back. It's all I need. Minimal casting play. A play that brings in money.'

'But not anymore,' said Macleod. 'They'll not continue the run, will they? Or do you think they will?'

'I doubt it. You're going to have to have somebody step in, but it won't happen for a couple of days. You don't make announcements like that. One would look cold, callous. The production company has to look after its own image now as well.'

'Where were you when he was shot?' asked Macleod.

'I was up in the lighting area.'

'And that is exactly where?'

'Well, if you're facing the stage, it's the furthest back from it you can get. I was sitting beside Dieter. He was doing the lights and the sound. I was giving a bit of help with that, but generally I was watching the play. Making sure on the first night in the new place that everything's in the right place. We have Julie and Peter in the wings, sorting out things like that from behind the stage, too.'

'So, you wouldn't have seen where the shot came from.'

'No. I just saw the direction he went after being shot. So I assumed it was off backstage left.'

'Are you planning on leaving Inverness?' asked Macleod.

'I am planning on going back to the hotel room and possibly picking up an enormous bottle of wine, and then waking up tomorrow to work out how on earth to keep this going. There's a slight chance. Turn it around, from a tragedy into a success story. The director who did unbelievably in the face of unknown horror. It's been a repeating story, trying to keep my career going.'

'You get some sleep,' said Macleod. 'May need to talk to you again. But thank you for your time.'

Frances shook hands with him as he left, and with Hope. When they got outside into the corridor, Macleod stopped for a moment.

'Not many people to see who did it, except the two backstage crew. We'll have to find out what they know.'

'This is where you're hiding yourself.'

Macleod looked up and saw a young Asian woman in a coverall suit. Jona gave him a smile. 'You up for a late-night discussion?'

'What have you got for me?'

'Come with me—and you're putting a suit on.'

Five minutes later, Macleod and Hope, dressed in coverall outfits, were standing with Jona on the stage.

'You see our body on the floor here,' she said. 'From what I can tell, the bullet that killed Angus came from the wings to the side of Helen. I think they call it backstage left in the business.'

'So, Angus would have seen who was shooting at him, would have seen somebody standing there with a gun?' said Hope.

'He never flinched,' said Macleod.

'Maybe it was the lights,' said Jona. 'Maybe his eyesight wasn't that good. I don't know yet. What I'm telling you is I think the shot came from over there. The interesting thing is that Helen would have been very close to it as well. It's a reasonably good shot not to hit her.'

'The shot's coming from over there,' said Macleod.

'Yes,' said Hope. 'So, we can discount everyone who's on the stage. So, our five actors can't do it, because the shot's coming from there.'

'But we don't see a shooter,' said Macleod. 'Nobody has talked about a shooter leaving. Nobody has talked about anybody coming out of here.'

'The backstage crew is then very important,' said Hope. 'If they saw something, or could it be them?'

'How good a shot?' asked Macleod.

'Shoot all the way across the stage like that, into the temple. It'd have to be a good shot,' said Jona. 'Ballistics can say more. I've asked for one to come in and give me some better advice. I know my basics, but I'm not the expert.'

'Can we be sure it's Angus they're shooting at?' asked Hope. 'You said Helen's quite close.'

'If you're trying to shoot somebody else, the only other reasonable explanation would be Helen. I think if I were shooting, and I'm no expert with a gun,' said Jona, 'I would hit either Helen or Angus with the shot. The others were standing too far away. It'd have to be a heck of a bad miss if you were aiming at any of the others.'

'The thing that bothers me,' said Macleod, 'is nobody talked about an escaping gunman. You've got to get away. The bullet's left in here. Probably quite lucky it didn't take out an audience member.'

'Very lucky,' said Jona.

'So, who's angry enough not to care about what happens to anybody else around him? It doesn't seem like a trained killer, does it?'

'You've also got yourself backstage. How do you know you can get out? Why shoot him on stage? What's being said? There's nothing being said, is there?' pondered Hope.

'Nobody's made a statement,' said Macleod. 'Nobody's come

forward. Nobody said Angus Morton is this, that or whatever. Although Sandra has said that there is potential in his past, although she's no evidence.'

'If you weren't there,' said Hope, 'they could just leave by the back though, couldn't they? You were the one who stopped the panic. You were the one who sent Clarissa off to shut everywhere down and not let anyone go.'

'We need to think about this,' said Macleod. 'Pull the team together. Make sure they've got other interviews done. Pull them together and let everybody else go home. It's been a long night. We need to get a game plan together. Get a line of attack.'

He watched Hope walk off to round up the others and stood with Jona looking at the body on the floor. There was a trail of crimson on the stage emanating from the head.

'I bet even you knew him,' said Jona. 'Angus Morton.'

'I'd heard of him,' said Macleod. 'But I'm not sure anybody knew him.'

'What does that mean?'

'Just something one of the other actors said. I need to go into his life to find a reason for this. That's never good. Not when the press are about. Not when it's somebody this famous. Getting reality from the fiction that gets printed. It's not easy.' Still, he turned and smiled at her. 'One last case. One last time.' Macleod turned and walked off the stage.

And Jona thought his shoulders were slumping. She'd never seen him so weary. Not this weary. As if he didn't want to take a case. And yet he had. She didn't have time, though, to think more. She had work to do.

Chapter 06

Macleod walked into the office of the theatre, generously offered by the management, and stood in the far corner, looking out of a window into the night below. There were many lights out there, cordons of press. He could see TV cameras rolling.

It was already on the news; already, reports of the death of Angus Morton were being flashed everywhere. Of course, the police hadn't said it was Angus Morton yet. They'd do that shortly after formal identification. But a man had been shot on stage, and everyone knew who it was. There had been an audience after all.

There was a knock on the door, and Hope entered, saying everyone would be there in a couple of minutes. She perched herself on the side of a desk, took out her mobile and placed a quick call. Macleod heard her talking to John but tried to ignore the words she was saying. He picked up his own mobile phone, thinking he should have phoned Jane by now, but there was a text message already there.

I'm fine, don't worry about me; get done what you need to get done. Emmett and Sabine have been good. Frank's here. They're all staying the night. I'm fine.

That was one thing off his mind. He realised that when it had happened, he'd gone on automatic pilot. He'd basically left Jane sitting there. And it must have been a heck of a shock to her. And yet she still tried to help. There was a tenacity to the woman that surprised him but that he loved. She was no cowering flower. She didn't hide away from things. But obviously she didn't have the practiced stomach for such an incident.

He would need to keep an eye on her over the next few months. Make sure she was okay. Nothing worse than seeing something like that and not getting help. It ate at you. It would eat away inside.

Perry and Susan arrived, gave him a nod but said nothing, standing up against the wall at the side. Ross soon followed, as ever, carrying his laptop. Macleod was about to start when he realised Clarissa wasn't there, and neither was Jona. The Asian woman arrived bang on the time they'd set for the meeting. But still no Clarissa.

'Anybody know where she is?' asked Macleod.

'She said she had to go out to the car park.'

There was a knock on the door. Before Macleod could say anything, it opened and a uniformed constable came in, carrying coffees, followed by Clarissa. He placed them down on the table, and she thanked him before he disappeared out of the room. Closing the door, Macleod looked over at her.

'You got coffee at this time?' He looked at his watch. 'It's almost five in the morning.'

'It's not great,' she said. 'Garage was open; it's one of those machines, but it's caffeine and you needed it. We needed it, and you were all way too busy. And you haven't got a proper place set up yet with the coffee and everything. So I thought,

I'll just sort it out. Team have enough to do.'

She picked up a cup and handed it over to Macleod. He took a sip, and she quizzed him with her eyes. 'It's fine,' he said, and she raised her eyebrows. 'Well, no, it's not fine. It's one of those machine ones, but it's hot and it's got caffeine and it's going in,' he said. 'So, thank you. Good of you to think of it.'

He stepped back, and Clarissa handed out the rest of the coffees. Once they had them in hand, Macleod turned to Jona.

'Can you run us through what you think happened?'

'Angus Morton was shot on stage. We know that. We've got how many witnesses to it? The bullet has come from backstage left,' she said. 'He is standing more towards upstage right. The bullet went through his head and out the back and embedded itself just underneath the box next to the start of the circle.'

'That box was full, wasn't it?' asked Macleod.

'It was.'

'Who was in it?'

Hope looked around and then Ross said, 'According to my records, or rather the records of the house, the tickets were bought by a local businessman.'

'Yes,' said Perry. 'Uniform interviewed him. He's here with his wife and a couple of other friends. Noticed nothing particular about him.'

'We're assuming at the moment,' said Macleod, 'that the bullet was for Angus Morton. But that's not proven. It could be for others. Check the businessman out,' said Macleod. 'Just make sure there's nothing untoward that we're glossing over and missing.'

'Will do,' said Ross.

'As I was saying,' continued Jona, 'the bullet's come from backstage left. Not quite sure how far. I've got a ballistics expert coming in to help me with that.'

'How does nobody see him?' asked Macleod. 'How does nobody see the shooter? The wings aren't that dark if you're on stage, are they? I mean, you have to see. When you act, you must be able to see. So, our backstage crew, they would know, wouldn't they?'

'The audience, according to Uniform, said there was a flash. There was definitely a flash, and it was beyond Helen,' said Perry. 'Helen was on stage, close to the line. Those on the far side of the theatre, and indeed up in the boxes, saw a flash. That's why I remember that man, the businessman in the box. He made a statement; said he saw a flash.'

'What about our two backstage? Frances Jollye, the director, is up at the lighting desk along with Dieter. Nothing suggested she's back there, but what about our two stagehands?'

'They weren't in that section,' said Susan. They were on the other side, backstage right.'

'Could they not see then?'

'You've got drapes coming down,' said Jona. 'What you can see from different parts of the stage depends on exactly where you are. You can't see the entire wings from the back. Can't see everything. You can see bits here, there and whatever. At the end of the day, they're trying to disguise the wings. You don't want to be able to see into them as the audience. Not well. The fact they've seen the flash shows that the shooter had to be on that line. You had to have a line from the wings to shoot.'

'I'm still not convinced that nobody saw them,' said Macleod.

'What about looking at this from the other angle?' said Hope. 'What about Angus's past? We need to get a motive, or are we just looking at a nut job?'

'Ross, what have you got on him?' asked Macleod.

'Very brief search, lots of rumours online, I mean lots of rumours, but there's no conclusive proof. Nothing concrete ever came of the allegations against him. The man's a national treasure. I know that's a corny word,' said Ross, 'but he's a national treasure. You don't become a national treasure if there's something obvious in your past.'

'You don't get shot dead on stage either,' said Macleod, 'unless there's something. We're going to need to do the digging, Ross. Look and find out what's happening. We need you to look at the other actors too, to find out when he worked with them before. Get details? When you talk about rumours, what are they?'

'The usual theatre thing. Young girls. Gambling, careless with money, buying up parts, making a name for himself, drink, alcohol, drugs, booze. I mean, they're rumours, unsubstantiated. They're just rumours, and they're all over the place. It's like picking up muck and just seeing what sticks. There's none of them I would turn around and say are worth pursuing now. I need to get into them. I need to see which has the potential to be true. At the moment, I wouldn't say any justify what's happened.'

'Fine,' said Macleod. 'Well, get into them, and get into them quick. If there was a shooter and they disappeared out the door, we will not find them unless we go through Angus's life.'

'Well, thanks very much,' said Jona. 'I might come up with something as I've got the bullet. I can maybe trace it. We might work out what type of gun it's come from. We can also—'

'I wasn't being disparaging,' said Macleod. 'But if they've gone out with the gun, we'll probably never see the gun again. They'll dump it somewhere, bury it. So, we'll need to trawl the

CCTV, see if anyone was departing or hanging about. We'll need to look at the CCTV from the surrounding streets, see who got away. But it's Inverness in the evening. Plenty of people about. To tag that they've been in the theatre will be difficult.'

'Can look and see if anybody's come in and then gone out again,' said Hope.

'Look,' said Macleod, 'the other thing is, the press will be all over this. Not a word. Not a word to them.'

'I threw one out earlier on,' said Clarissa. 'Cheeky bugger, got my toe up his backside.'

'I really hope that's a figure of speech,' said Macleod.

Clarissa shook her shoulders, causing Perry to nearly burst out laughing.

'Perry,' said Macleod, 'I want you and Susan to follow Rupert back to the hotel, but at a distance. He's too keen to get back. I want to see why. Something's not sitting right with him. The others, their reaction, seems fair enough.'

'You realise something, don't you?' asked Perry.

'What?' asked Macleod.

'Normally when we interview people, they're ordinary people, and you just take their reaction as being what they are. It's very hard to fake a reaction, certainly a convincing one. However, we're dealing with people who, by their very nature, can fake a reaction.'

'Actors,' said Susan, 'we're dealing with a load of actors. How do you know what they're saying is true? How do you know the way they're behaving is true?'

'By getting the facts, getting the details, picking the holes, same as we do with anyone else,' said Macleod. 'Now, if we're going to find out if anybody should have seen the shooter, we're going to need to know exactly where everybody was. We're going to have to walk through the last minutes. Hope, that's your job. You're going to assemble the details that show us where everybody was. See who has cover from who. See who's talking, whose ideas match up, who saw who, and when. And let's get the script. Let's see where everybody was meant to be. That's the other thing. They've rehearsed this so that everybody should have a role and should have a position.'

'Let's get on it,' said Hope.

Macleod turned to Clarissa. 'And you can head home, pick Frank up; he's at my house.'

'You sure?' she asked. 'This isn't because I brought you coffee that wasn't up to your usual standard.'

'Hang on a minute,' he said. 'Rest of you, off you go, get sorted. Ross, once you get the place secured and an ongoing presence, we're going to head back and run things from Hope's office. No need to be camped out here; we're only down the road by a couple of minutes.'

'Yes, sir,' said Ross. Slowly, everyone faded out, Hope the last, glancing at Macleod just to check that she wasn't required. With the door closed, Macleod turned to Clarissa.

'Well done tonight,' he said, 'but you need to go.'

'If Hope needs help—'

'Hope's not running the case. I am.'

'Why? You're leaving soon. She needs to stand on her own feet.'

'She can stand on her own feet, but she doesn't need this. You've seen these cases before, seen the big ones. You've seen what they can do to people. Especially if it doesn't work out in your favour, if things don't get solved. They linger with you.'

'And what?' said Clarissa. 'You want it to linger with you? If this drags on, you're not going to be able to leave. And forgive me for saying so, but you need out.'

'I know I need out. I have felt that coming for a while. Jane needs me out. You need out too at some point,' he said. 'We're not getting any younger.'

'No,' said Clarissa. 'But when it happened tonight, who's there? You and me.'

'Do you think anybody got out? Do you think the gunman could have left before you closed everywhere off?'

'Of course he could,' said Clarissa. 'I was quick. I was fast, and I held the audience members in. Maybe one of them snuck out of a seat round the back?'

'No, I'm not going for that. If you wanted to kill him, you wouldn't do it on the stage. Unless you're trying to make a statement. And no statement has been made,' said Macleod. 'You're killing him on the stage because you know how things work and you can find yourself an opportunity, or you're making a statement. Otherwise, you'd kill him out in the open. Easier to get away. You don't kill somebody when you're trapped, especially in a backstage situation. There's something about this. Something clever. There's something that says, this is why we've done it here. Why now? And not a statement. Maybe that's because the reason doesn't require a statement.'

'Simple revenge,' said Clarissa.

'Possible. You know what it's like. Could be more than one reason.'

'If you need me, just call.'

'Go by mine, pick up Frank. Emmett and Sabina are with Jane. You get some sleep. Let them look after Jane. I'll be back sometime.'

'Who are you kidding?' said Clarissa. She left, leaving

Macleod alone in the room.

His shoulders were sore. He was tired. And the office was cool. The coffee had been very welcome. Yes, it tasted like rubbish, but it was warm. He'd need to get some warmth into him. Soup would be a good idea at some point. When he got back to the station, he'd have some of that soup. Get a meal. He needed to eat. He hadn't eaten all night.

Something was bugging him, though. No one had seen the shooter. Not a sign. Nobody said, 'Oh, it might have been a six-foot man, but we couldn't see properly.' It was all just nobody saw. Just a flash. What was it then? What was bugging him? Like a trick he wasn't seeing. He shrugged his shoulders. It would come. He walked over to the window and looked out. There they were, the dogs needing a story. They wouldn't go. He needed to feed them. It was time to talk to the press.

Chapter 07

'You think there'll be daylight soon?'

'Why—are you scared in the dark?' asked Perry.

Susan glanced over at him. 'It's easier trailing in the dark when all they can see is a pair of headlights,' she said. 'It's harder in daylight.'

'Well, there's the taxi,' said Perry. They were sitting parked across the street and watched as Rupert was led through a press pack by some officers and put into a taxi. Susan started the car and followed the taxi back to the Inverness hotel that was accommodating the cast.

Rupert was the last one to go, Sandra having been given priority as the most senior actor before the awaiting taxis being filtered down. The stage crew had gone off to get their own, for they weren't faces that the press knew. Being the last, Rupert arrived at the hotel after everyone else.

Susan parked in the car park, Perry telling her to wait while he followed inside, just to make sure Rupert went to his room. The hotel lobby was large and, as such, while it was quiet, Perry was able to remain out of sight. He went through the revolving door, about thirty seconds after Rupert, and then stood near a plant pot while Rupert headed into the bar area. It was closed, the hour being early, and Rupert came out swearing.

The night clerk appeared from his room behind the main desk. 'Can I help you, sir?'

'You can get me a drink,' said Rupert. The night clerk was maybe in his thirties, dressed in a smart waistcoat with a cravat.

'I'm afraid not; it's beyond licensing hours, sir.'

'It's a bar, there's nobody else here, no one's going to care. Here!' Rupert reached inside and pulled out some notes.

'The bar is closed. I can't get you anything from the bar. We have a night menu. I can get you food. We can do coffee. I could get you a soft drink, but I'm not permitted to sell alcohol.'

'All I want's a damn drink. It's a bloody drink. We're paying you guys enough to be here. Paying you enough to live in this place. Bloody hell. We wouldn't get this in London.'

'As I said, sir, licensing laws are very strict. I would lose my job for serving you.'

'Bloody hell,' said Rupert. He turned and kicked a table. The night clerk didn't flinch. Rupert sat down for a moment, then he walked over towards the bar. The night clerk stood impassive behind the desk, while Perry lingered, unseen by the night clerk so far. Rupert came back.

'Where's the bloody key? Let's get that place open.'

'Told you, sir, we can't serve. I can get you a coffee or a soft drink, a glass of water. I cannot serve you alcohol.'

'I'll break the bloody place down.'

'You do that, sir, I'll be forced to call the police.'

'Bastard,' said Rupert. He stormed around for a moment. 'There won't be any bloody police anyway, not after what's happened.'

'Terribly sorry for that, sir, but it doesn't change the fact that I can't—'

'You can't even serve a bloody drink!' Rupert swore loudly. 'Bloody coffee then, get me a bloody coffee!'

'Very good, sir,' said the night clerk. He disappeared into the bar area while Rupert went and sat down in front of the fire. It was a very moderate fire, kept going enough for the lobby to be at a reasonable heat. As the night clerk returned with the coffee, placing it down on the table beside Rupert, Rupert muttered at him, and Perry watched as the man chucked a few more logs on the fire.

It soon picked up heat, blazing out, and the night clerk went back to his desk. He didn't disappear into the back room, Perry noted, but monitored his guest. Not surprisingly, as Perry would have kept an eye on him. Who knew what the man might do?

Perry slid in behind one of the curtains and was only twenty feet away from Rupert. He watched him take out his phone and begin ringing.

'Pick up, pick up, come on,' said Rupert.

Perry wondered what he was so anxious about, but the man was clearly tense, as well as angry. He was also somewhat drunk, because he didn't keep the level of his voice at a reasonable volume. He wasn't quite shouting, but he was definitely louder than he should have been, for being on a phone.

'Jerry,' said Rupert suddenly, 'you need to watch your back. You've got to stay stum. You've got to make sure that they don't say anything. He's dead. Somebody shot him. Bloody hell. Somebody shot him. Pay them off. All right? You'll need to pay them off, Jerry. Yes, I know, but pay them off. Can't have this lingering about. Needs to go away very, very quickly. I can't be dealing with it, can I? Press are everywhere. My face is on these posters. I'm part of the production. They know who I am. I get seen anywhere with that, it's going to get plastered everywhere. You know what's going to happen? You know what's happening now? You're going to get rumours. Loads and loads of rumours. And we're not getting caught up in this. We're getting out. Out now. Out and away. Okay? Just deal with it, Jerry. Sort it out. Okay? Of course I've got money.'

Rupert put the phone down, and Perry watched as he swore under his breath. He picked up the coffee again, found it to be empty, and turned and glared at the night clerk.

'I take it I can access my minibar.'

'Of course, sir. What you do in your room is up to you. I just can't serve any alcohol from the bar outside of licensed hours.'

Rupert swore again and marched over to a lift. Pressing it, he grumbled until the doors opened. He half stumbled in. Perry watched him press a button, and he estimated him to be on about floor three. When the doors closed and the lift was moving up, Perry stepped out from behind the curtain.

The night clerk gasped. 'Sir? Were you listening in? How long have you been there, sir?'

Perry reached inside his jacket, pulled out his ID, and held it up to the night clerk. 'Bit of an awkward customer. Been involved in the unfortunate circumstances tonight. I'm just making sure that he got back safely without any press about. He doesn't need to know I was here. No one needs to know I was here. In particular, you need to forget I was here. I'm sure you can do that for me.'

'Well, that's understood. Very good of you to keep an eye on him.'

'Of course, there might be a lot of press coming around. Don't talk to them. Make sure they stay out of the lobby here. You're probably going to get some police on the doors, especially if a lot of press turn up. If you get anybody now, phone the station. Okay? And just tell them the press has been around the hotel; we'll deal with it from there on. Thank you for your help and well done with the bar. You're absolutely right; you can't serve him.'

Perry turned and walked out, having given a good reason to be there. He walked across the car park and got into the passenger seat beside Susan, who was still in the driver's chair. She had the radio on and was listening but turned it down as Perry entered the car.

'Well, we need to keep a watch. He spoke to some guy called Jerry. They're needing to keep something quiet, talked about a bit of money being available, but things had to be kept stum, dealt with.'

'Great,' said Susan. She gave a yawn.

'I can take first watch if you want,' said Perry.

'No,' said Susan. 'You have a sleep. I'm okay.'

Perry nodded, got out of the car and then got into the back seat. He took off his jacket and lay down. Awkwardly, he got his shoes off, pulling his legs up tight. The seat was big enough for Perry to be on, but he couldn't move easily for fear of falling down into the footwell. He pulled his jacket over himself. There was silence in the car for a bit, Susan, letting the radio remain fairly quiet.

'Perry,' she said. 'How would you feel if I moved on?'

'Moved on?' queried Perry. 'Why are you moving on?'

'Seoras spoke to me. He floated the idea that I might join Emmett.'

'Is that what you want? Cold cases? It's not as dynamic. It's not as—'

'No, but it would . . . well, things aren't the same between you and me, are they? Things aren't the way they used to be, now that you're with Tanya.'

'Don't move on because of me,' said Perry. 'I can work with you. It's fine. I can work with you. You know, I don't have a problem with it. We said our piece. Things didn't work out.'

'Things didn't work out because I didn't let them,' said Susan. 'I kick myself, Perry. Understand that. And every time I work with you here, I kick myself. If I work with Emmett, I'll probably still kick myself when I think about it, but I won't have you to look at every day. I won't have the reminder that I blew it.'

'That's not fair, is it?' said Perry. 'I mean, we blew it.'

'Perry, stop being nice. I blew it. You were ready. You wanted me. I said no. I kept you at arm's length. I kept you away for so long. And then, well, Tanya's come and I'm happy for you. Yes, I am. I am, but I'm kicking myself.'

'Well, I don't want you to be uncomfortable. I don't want you to be—'

'Perry, you're being too damn reasonable. You're always so damn reasonable. It's what's so nice about you.'

'I can't help being who I am.'

'No, you can't,' said Susan. 'And that's why it won't work, you and me. Not day in, day out. Not partnering up. If, well, if Sabine comes across, Macleod said that would work. Sabine needs to move anyway. Seoras said that she and Emmett are, well . . .'

'Yes, she's got a thing for Emmett,' said Perry.

'How did you know?' asked Susan.

'Come on,' said Perry. 'Not that difficult to read.'

'It's damn difficult to read. How do you do that? How do

you—'

Perry shrugged his shoulders. 'You want to move on? Move on,' said Perry. 'If it makes you happier. If it makes you—'

'It doesn't make me happy but it'll make me function. It'll make me . . . hopefully, make me move on. You have. I haven't.'

'Sorry,' said Perry. 'If I could have made it easier. If I could have—'

'It's not your fault. This is what I mean. Every time I try to tell you I'm struggling, it's me, it's me that's done it, you apologise. You just remind me why I kick myself, why I'm annoyed I blew it. You're a good man, Perry, and I'm not good at picking good men. It took me long enough to realise you were the one I should pick. And then I was too late. I've got to get better at that. I've picked some arseholes in my time.'

'We live and learn,' said Perry. 'Everybody makes mistakes. Everybody blows it. Everybody.'

'Shut up, Perry,' said Susan. 'You can't make me feel better about this. I just have to move on.'

'I don't want to lose you as a friend,' said Perry.

'You won't. We can be friends. We can say hello and whatever. But I'll never get past the bit that I blew it. It's just easier if I don't work so closely with you. Who knows? Maybe I'll find another Perry somewhere.'

'Might find somebody better.'

Susan sat looking out of the car, the cold car park before her, the sun only barely threatening to come up. Typical Perry. 'You might find somebody better,' he says. Downplaying himself. She could feel a tear in her eye but was glad he couldn't see it. She probably shouldn't have brought it up.

Susan doubted he was sleeping now. He was probably lying there, thinking about how he could best help her move on.

How he could best assist. This was the problem. It wasn't anything Perry did wrong. It was everything he did right that just brought it all back to her. She'd make the move. She had to. It was only fair to him and the only thing that was fair to herself. She hoped he would get to sleep soon because the silence with him being awake was killing her.

Chapter 08

Macleod dipped his spoon into the soup, lifted it and felt the heat on his tongue. He sat, feeding himself, savouring every drop of mushroom that passed his lips. He broke a small roll apart, dipped it into the soup and chewed on it.

The chill in his bones was gradually slipping away. He was feeling it now. Bitter days and even colder nights seemed to seep into him more. He'd have to wear thermals. It was an age thing, wasn't it? He'd need to do it, though. Need to abandon himself to the comforts that so often the male ego refuses to accept.

Maybe it wasn't the cold, though. Maybe it was just being up for so long. That played a part too, didn't it? That kind of tiredness would make you feel cold. He reached and grabbed the coffee in front of him. It was from the canteen, and it wasn't terrific, but again, it was hot. All he wanted was heat. He felt the vibration on his phone and picked it up, smiling when he saw the message.

Keep going. Last one. Keep going.

The thing about Jane was she knew how to reach him. She knew how to get under the skin. Unlike most on the team,

Jane had known he was ready, ready to throw in the towel. Well, that was a terrible expression. She'd told him that. He wasn't throwing in the towel. He was walking out with his head held high.

Well, he'd see about that after this case. He was on a hiding-to-nothing with this. He either blew apart a nation's love of a national treasure, or you point out how senselessly he's died. Either way, it wasn't a good news story.

There'd been plenty fallen after all, plenty of figures from back in the day who had fallen down because of past transgressions. Macleod didn't share any pity with some of them. Some of what they did was monstrous, but the childhood dream, the memories of so many people had been shattered. You didn't know at the time who you were looking up to, and neither did your parents, or they would have railed against it. Just what was he looking into now?

Ross would find out, though, would dig out the truth from the rumour. Ross's place, the online world, the new battlefield. He was good at that.

Macleod felt his phone vibrate again. Hope was ready for him, apparently. He tapped in he'd be five minutes and got back to work on his soup. By the time he stood to go upstairs, he was feeling somewhat revived. As he climbed those stairs, he didn't know what he was feeling. Last time though. Last time on the job. Last time running it. He knew Hope was annoyed with him for it, but she'd agreed to his better judgement.

Or had she just let the old fool have one more go? He wasn't very sure. He didn't want to fall out with her. That wouldn't happen, anyway. There was plenty in this life for her to fall out with him over that she hadn't done. Part of him wanted to send her home for an hour. See the little one. That would be interfering. And maybe as a godfather he had a right to interfere, but not as her boss. She needed to find the balance between work and the little one. That was her job, not his.

He knocked on the door and got a pleasant 'Come in' and saw her standing over by a large whiteboard. She looked fresh, which told him the difference between the two of them. Hope was in blue jeans and a black t-shirt, the red hair in a ponytail since she was working. She gave a smile as he came in.

'You all right?'

'No, knackered, cold to the core. You look your usual sprightly self.'

'Hunt's on,' she said. He knew what she meant. But not that long ago, he would have felt that fire too. It wasn't there anymore. It wasn't. That bothered him. It was like something within him was dying. Something within him wasn't the same. It wasn't the mind, though. The mind was still sharp. He knew that. It was something else.

'What have you got for me?'

'Right. You're looking at the stage here,' she said, pointing to the whiteboard. 'They give position names for the actors. Okay, so if the actor is standing in the middle, he's centre stage; if the actor is off to the right as the audience looks at it, that's left, stage left. If he's on the right as he looks at it, it's stage right.'

'Okay, something like that, just point to where they all are.'

'Angus is centre stage, Helen Love is stage left, okay; that's because that's the main action is happening at this point. So, the shot comes just over the back of Helen. She's almost in line with it, okay. Sandra and Alistair are downstage right. They're well clear of the shot at the front.

'Frances, our director, had just come down from the lighting and sound box. She'd said to us she'd been up in the box, which is technically correct, but apparently she'd literally just left it and was standing just outside. Dieter was in the light and sound booth, the box as she called it. Julie and Peter are both in the wings, right?

'So, you've got Sandra and Alistair too far forward to be affected by the shot. Julie and Peter are stage right in the wings; therefore, they're too far back to be affected by the shot. The only people who can be affected by the shot are Angus and Helen. It goes just past Helen and hits Angus spot on. The shot comes from offstage, in the wings. Upstage, left, in the wings. The crew's all accounted for. Nobody in the crew is where that shot comes from.'

'So, there must be someone else,' said Macleod. 'Or somebody's lying.'

'Nobody's lying,' said Hope. 'Actors are on stage. Can't get away from that. I went over the statements, and you saw it yourself. All the actors are on stage. So, they're there. That's a fact. Frances, just outside the box, in the box previously. Dieter says so, and some of the audience have said it as well. They were in the rear. They remember her stepping down and coming out just to the front.'

'But what about our stage crew? You said they were both in the wings on the right. How do we know? They could just be saying that. I assume they're the only two people who know they're there.'

'No, Helen knows they're there. Helen can see them. Helen says they're there. Nobody else can see them from the stage. Downstage right is too far away from them. You'd have to be looking over your shoulder so you can't see.'

'Okay. And the shot comes from off the stage by Helen.'

'I've gone through the statements,' said Hope. 'The flash of light comes from there. Jona says the trajectory of the bullet is coming from there, so that all ties up. We have got nobody else seen backstage coming up to that point.'

'Someone's got to be sneaked in quickly.'

'Well, that's where you get a problem,' said Hope. 'That's where I've got a big problem.'

'Why?' asked Macleod.

'When it comes to the time for the performance, and with it being Angus Morton, those who run Ness Theatre went into what they called locking down the stage area. So, prior to the play beginning, about two or three minutes beforehand, the house manager blocks off everywhere with staff. So, there is staff there to stop anyone going backstage. It's not that they think he's going to be attacked; it's that they don't want people wandering around in the wrong place. From that point until the actual incident, nobody could have got through.

'During the interval, the staff remained there as well. The staff rotated once during that time, but never was the access to backstage open for anyone. No one could have sneaked through, or at least it doesn't look like they did.'

'What about coming in from the rear?'

'Again, locked up because of the press, etc. There are fire doors, but none were shown as being open.'

'So, hang on a minute,' said Macleod, 'what about coming in through the stage, what about half time at the interval?'

'They would kick up a fuss if somebody snuck in, and you've got the safety curtain come down as well, according to the house manager.'

'Someone has to be there,' says Macleod, 'someone has to be there because a gunshot was fired, so somebody had a gun, shot it, and then got rid of it, legged it out of there.'

'Clarissa saw no one except the stage crew.'

'I'm not fathoming this,' said Macleod.

'I think you are,' said Hope. 'It's just a mystery.'

'No, that doesn't happen. Do we have anywhere that people can hide? Under the stage?'

'Stage is checked beforehand. Nobody got in. We are talking about a reasonably sealed unit here. They're worried because of who you've got up there. Angus Morton. They don't want anybody coming in and messing it up. Things happen. So, there's security. It's not unbelievably tight, but it's decent. You'd certainly notice anybody sneaking about. And there are no reports of that.'

'Any way in from the outside? Any tunnels? Anything like that?'

There was a knock at the door. Hope walked over and opened the office door to find Jona standing outside.

'Come in. Come in,' said Hope.

Jona looked over at the whiteboard. 'Oh, somebody's been busy.'

'You got something to tell us?' asked Macleod.

'Angus Morton was shot through the head. And the shot comes from offstage, akin to the upstage left position. I can't say how far back it comes from. With the speed at which the bullet has been travelling, we can't be precise. But it's from this position over here. The ballistics expert said yes, he could trace the bullet to the gun, if we can find the gun. However, he reckoned it's a pretty decent shot.'

'Anything else about it?' asked Macleod.

'Only one thing. Doesn't seem to be at the height of an adult. They may have knelt to shoot. One leg in front, one knee down job, not prone on the floor. But the height wouldn't have been a standing adult.'

'And you would do that because?'

'Well, maybe it's to brace yourself. At the end of the day, if a gun fires, it's going to kick back.'

'Question,' said Hope. 'Would you do that if you're trained with a firearm? Or untrained? Or minimal training? What goes through your head to say I'm going to go down on the knee? Professional?'

'Not professional,' said Jona. 'Professionals want to be out of there quickly. They will not kneel because, looking at where it is, you can take that shot standing up. They can brace themselves differently. You don't need to go down on a knee to do it.'

'So what are we left with?' said Macleod. 'A killer with a gun that nobody sees, come in, but technically can't get in, and then nobody sees going out.'

'I need to scan some more of these statements to trace where the killer might have gone,' said Hope. 'To see if there's anybody on their way, moving away from the area.'

'That's going to be hard,' said Macleod. 'The place was in chaos. You had somebody being shot, all eyes on the stage waiting for the play to finish. Only a few people, like myself, Clarissa, and people who knew gunshots, reacted straight away to the real gunshot.'

'Did they come out the front?' asked Hope. 'Do you think there's any way that—?'

'Nobody came off that stage,' said Macleod. 'I stood up as soon as the shot happened, came down one side, and was watching the stage. Clarissa was doing the same from the other side. Nobody came off the front of the stage. I was on the stage afterwards. Nobody came off, but there was nobody in the wings. Clarissa went into those wings, couldn't find anyone, so they must have legged it by then. Took me a minute or just a little over a minute to get up there, a bit of panic, hard to get out of the row because I was sat in the middle.'

'So, the conundrum remains. How did they get in without being seen? And how did they get out without being seen?' asked Hope.

'It also means that we've got a problem,' said Macleod, 'because we've got nothing on the killer. We're going to have to find the killer another way. We need to find out why Morton's dead.'

'Well, I believe he was the one they meant to kill. Anyone who's a decent shot,' said Jona, 'would have taken out Helen Love. She's the only other one near the line of fire.'

'Would it be hard to miss her if you were an amateur?' asked Macleod.

'Yes, steady hands. Very steady hands. It's a pretty crisp shot to pass her by. I reckon the bullet must have passed within a couple of inches of her shoulder.'

Macleod thought for a moment. 'Something else,' he said. 'There must be something else. Somebody must have seen them, seen how it was done. Somebody must have seen them coming in.'

There was a knock at the door.

'Anybody else invited to the party? I mean, it's getting good in here,' said Hope. She marched over and opened the door. 'Alan,' she said.

'Got something for you,' he said. 'Sir, you're going to like this.' Macleod wasn't so sure, but he was ready for any new information.

Chapter 09

'It'll be easier if you come to my desk,' said Ross. Macleod nodded and let the two women exit first, Jona disappearing off to her own section. Hope followed Ross to his desk, and Macleod could see there were a myriad of papers on it. Print-offs here, there, and everywhere. That wasn't usual for Ross. Ross liked to be neat, but he'd clearly been at this for a while.

'You've been cross-referencing stuff.'

'I haven't got on to that yet,' said Ross, almost testily. 'This is just information indicating possible motives.'

'You going to write a book after?' said Hope.

'You said he's a national treasure,' said Ross, 'that might be his public persona; he's certainly not a national treasure to everyone.'

'What do you mean?' asked Macleod.

Ross picked up some of the papers, and held them up in front of him. 'There are tenuous links to organised crime, especially around Glasgow,' said Ross.

'What sort of crime around Glasgow?'

'The Jamesons.'

Macleod's face fell. 'Not the Jamesons—surely not the Jamesons.'

'The Jamesons,' said Hope, 'they're one of the bigger crime families, aren't they?'

'Quite old. They go back,' said Macleod. 'How tenuous are these links?'

'Not very tenuous. I can't prove any of them, but there are instances of Morton talking to them and being seen with them. In nightclubs and other places, but not nightclubs you'd take your daughter to.'

'Okay,' said Macleod. 'What else?' Ross put down the papers he was holding and picked up a different pile.

'Animal rights activists want to take him out. He says there's nothing like beef. Aberdeen Angus beef. Any type of beef, really. As long as it's Scottish. Big promoter of it, but he's said a few other things. Called vegetarians nutters, vegans lunatics. Not out in the national press, though. Quieter. A lot of it was hushed up. He seems to have a heck of a PR agent,' said Ross.

'I don't buy it's them,' said Macleod.

'No,' said Hope. 'That would be out by now. It's quite an extreme act for people of that persuasion, although there are groups who would do it, but they would tell you. They would lord it over everybody, pointing out the animal that he was.'

'A lot of threats, though,' said Ross. 'Not sure you can discount it completely.' He put that pile down and picked up another one. 'There's a report of a father threatening to kill Angus as he was having an unsubstantiated affair with his young son.'

'Really? How unsubstantiated?'

'There's nothing concrete. There's no proof of meetings, no proof they've ever been together, but the father is going off on one in all the reports.'

'Okay. What else we got?' asked Macleod, realising that not all the paper had been picked up by Ross yet. Ross put down that particular pile and grabbed another pile.

'Evidence of gambling—unpaid debts to a known illegal gambling syndicate. I wouldn't say these are tenuous. I'd say these are proof, but not courtroom proof. You would say this would be accepted, just not watertight in a court of law.'

'Really?' said Macleod. 'Bank account showing it?'

'Bank accounts are awkward. This is the bank account he seems to operate out of, and it all looks fine. I'm not sure that's all of his bank accounts, though. I'm digging to find some other funds.'

'Good,' said Macleod. 'That's a great start.'

'What do we do with it though?' asked Hope.

'Well, we need to look at each of them,' said Macleod. 'We have got nothing else to go on at the moment. We're struggling with our shooter. So, let's open up our victim. We'll leave the animal rights activists at the moment. I don't think it's them. They haven't shouted, but if they do, we'll get on to it.'

'Perry and Susan—what's the deal with them at the moment?' Macleod asked Hope.

'They still say they need to trace who Rupert was talking to. That's something we need to keep tabs on. He hasn't moved from the hotel yet.'

'Well, keep them on that,' said Macleod. 'Gambling syndicate, let's get Clarissa on that.'

'Clarissa?' asked Ross, raising an eyebrow.

'I want you here, and I want you buried in your computer, and I want you pulling out every bit of information you can find. Cross-referencing like you do, that's where you're going to serve me best at the moment, Ross.'

'Okay. That leaves Hope and me. We'll need extra people in on this one. Gambling syndicate's a good one for Clarissa. There's reasonable proof, but not enough. Clarissa can walk in there and work out what's what. I'm not convinced a gambling syndicate's going to take it out on him in this way. It'd be much more subtle than that. It would be a professional hit. What's the possibility of this being such a hit? I don't like that the shooter puts himself in that position. That's not a pro hit. Easier to shoot him elsewhere.

'At the end of the day, if it's a gambling issue, they would have to get to a point of giving up getting the money back. Because if you're going to shoot him, it's a testimony to other people, don't mess with us or you're dead,' said Macleod. 'So, they would be at the end of their tether. Clarissa can shake that down.'

'So, I'll look at the father,' said Hope.

'No,' said Macleod, 'don't. Let's get Patterson to look at the father. We need to bring extra people in.'

'What about Emmett?' asked Hope.

'Keep it with Patterson; it's a lower level. We don't want to spook the father. At the end of the day, he's saying there's an issue. We don't want the press to see me sending all my detective inspectors everywhere. They'll look at where you're going, what you're doing. A crime syndicate will not shout to the press, but this man might. And I don't want us to be in the middle of that if he does. It may just be a nothing story. Patterson will attract less attention from the press, but he's thorough.'

'So what do you want me to do?' asked Hope.

'You need to stay here and direct,' said Macleod. 'I'm going to see the Jamesons in Glasgow.'

'Is that wise? I mean, on your own? Not a friendly bunch of people you're going to.'

'No, it's not,' said Macleod. 'And if I go down there with everyone, they'll think something's really up. At the moment, if I go on my own, I might get something out of the old man. We go back. We've had dealings, and not all of them have been without benefit to each other.'

'Sir?' asked Ross.

'Sometimes lines cross, Ross. I did nothing illegal, and I did nothing for them that hurt other people deliberately. But sometimes in doing the right thing, it actually benefits them as well. Sometimes, especially when the gangs are at each other's throats, you have to work out the best path. It's not simple. Thank you, Ross.'

Macleod started walking back towards Hope's office, and she followed him. Once inside, he closed the door.

'I want to see the Jamesons because I have a link. They know I'm retiring soon. I mean, everybody knows it because word gets around. I might get something out of them they wouldn't say otherwise, especially if they're not actually involved. Might get more of an idea about the man, if he spent time with them. I'm best doing that on my own. If I go with you, they'll not open up the same.'

Hope looked at him, not quite following.

'You might have the looks, but you'll still be here after this case is done, and they'll not be happy to hand over information like that. I'll be out of here and gone, and they owe me. I've saved some of their backsides in the past. Not by giving them information we shouldn't, but by actually stopping people from killing them.'

'You going to be long?' asked Hope.

'See where it leads,' said Macleod. 'But you need to be here. We need to keep on top of the press. You'll have to feed reasonable updates to them, even though there isn't anything, because if you don't feed them, they get nasty and start printing things that really aren't true. I also need somebody here looking after Perry and the gang.'

Macleod looked over at the whiteboard again. 'Go through the statements. See if you can see anybody around the stage we don't know about . But if not, we're going to have to look at this differently.'

'Differently? In what way?'

'I don't know. We have to look at it differently. The way we're looking at it at the moment isn't bringing up the answers to how he got shot, or who he got shot by.'

The phone rang. Hope ran across and then picked up. 'It's for you, Seoras,' she said. Macleod went over and listened before simply saying 'no' and putting the phone down.

'Who was that?'

'Scottish television news. They wanted me to come on and be interviewed about what happened. I mean, as if I'm going to do that.'

'Open policing.'

'Go on and say what,' said Macleod. 'Nothing. They want me for a special when I retire as well. They're not getting that either.'

'You'd better pack or get flights sorted if you're going to Glasgow. Are you going to drive down?'

'I'll fly,' said Macleod. 'And I'll not go with any uniform. I'll go on my own. See what I can learn. Hopefully be back tonight or the following day. Unless anything flows from the material

I get. Keep the rest of them at it. Love to the wee guy.'

'You think I'm going to see Ian before tomorrow morning?'

'You need to make time for—.' And then he stopped. 'You'll work it out.'

Hope grinned at him, and Macleod left, heading back up to his office. He saw Tanya, his secretary, at her desk and stopped by.

'Tanya, I'm heading down to Glasgow. Get me booked on the next flight down and get me a hire car at the other end. Nothing flash, basic run around.'

'Jane's been on just asking how you are—didn't want to disturb you directly.'

'Thank you.'

He headed for his office, and when he entered, he got behind his desk, sat down and picked up the phone. It was answered by Sabine, who called Jane to the phone.

'They're still there then?'

'We've had some phone calls and approaches from the press. Sabine and Emmett have dealt with it. Emmett's gone now. Sabine's here at the moment. Clarissa picked up Frank last night. Or rather, this morning.'

'Did you sleep okay?' asked Macleod.

'Not really. Kept seeing it.'

'That's to be expected. We can get you a shrink to talk to about it if it stays. But in the first week, it's pretty normal for it to run through your head.'

'What about you?'

'Well, I haven't slept,' said Macleod. 'But I'll be fine with that. You get used to it, to a degree.'

'I'm not sure I know how to get used to that.'

'You just do. I have to head off to Glasgow. See some people

I used to work with.'

'Former policemen.'

'Not quite. People I thought I'd never see again, but the case has brought it up.'

'You sound tired,' said Jane, concern in her voice.

'Been up all night.'

'Not that kind of tired. Sick of it. Fed up. Stop. Wanting to move on. You can give it to Hope. She's good enough. You keep telling me that.'

'She is good enough. But in this kind of case, well . . . this kind of case can haunt you and your career. I haven't helped her get up to where she is now to have her stuck because of something like this. It won't matter to me. I'm leaving. I'm off to do other things.'

'What about your legacy?'

'Legacy? When did you learn the word legacy? I couldn't care less about my legacy. I got into this to bang up people who did the wrong thing. To sort out messes. To stop people from killing other people. I don't look for a legacy.'

'You don't, do you?' said Jane. 'Be safe down there. You're nearly done. Be safe.'

'I will. And we'll go away. We'll go do that trip you want. That's definite. I'm not backing out of that. I will go with you. We'll see the world together. We'll live, Jane. Money isn't an issue. We can do it.'

'That's my man,' said Jane. 'Be safe. And did you eat?'

'Yes, I ate. If this keeps up, I'll need a couple of shirts, though. Give them to Sabine when she goes back into the office. She can pop them in to Tanya.'

'Good. Save me the trip.'

'I'll speak to you soon,' said Macleod. 'Love you.'

'Be safe. Love you too.'

He closed down the call and turned to look out the window. Stupid view. He really hated this view. He looked around his office. Ever since he moved up here, he never got used to the office. It wasn't his. His was downstairs. His was Hope's office. Except it wasn't. His office was gone. That detective inspector was gone. That was when Seoras the policeman started to die. He recognised it now. Yes, he'd gone on and done other things, but that was when he had been taken away, or rather sacrificed himself to be something else.

It was all for Hope to rise up, and there was no way now he was going to let that career be jeopardised by a case like this. There was a knock on the door. 'Come in,' said Macleod. Tanya entered with some papers in her hand. She put them down on the desk in front of Macleod.

'You've got an hour and a half; you need to get to Inverness Airport; I've got you the hire car booked, the details are all there. I've already booked you on the flight. That's your boarding pass. "Go!" as they say.'

'Somebody's going to get very lucky when they take over from me. Thanks, Tanya.'

'Give us a buzz if you need a hotel,' she said. 'I'll sort that out for you too. Do you want me to book one just in case?'

'I won't know where I'm going to be,' said Macleod. 'So, I'll speak to you if I need it.'

Tanya nodded, wished him a pleasant trip, and left him in the office. He checked he had his car keys, looked around and wondered what he should take with him. There was a grab bag: pants, socks, a shirt, some toiletries. He picked it up. It could be taken in the aircraft cabin so he wouldn't need to book luggage.

Luggage was a perk on most of the flights out of Inverness, especially if they were internal to Scotland. Putting on his coat, he gave a smile, looked around, and left for Glasgow.

Chapter 10

Perry had been in a deep sleep. It had been a particularly pleasant one. He'd been walking with Tanya and had been in an amorous mood. He'd gone to get her some coffee, and then at the shack that was serving the coffee, Perry had noticed that the server was Susan. She kept asking would he not come inside the shack, and Perry said no. She said that he'd once wanted to come into the shack, but he said he didn't want that anymore. She'd served him coffee, and he'd gone back with the coffee to Tanya. He was going back for a second coffee, about to speak to Susan once again, when he was suddenly woken up.

He rolled over, nearly dropping into the well between the front and rear seats of the car, his face half-mashed against the seat in front of him.

'What on earth?'

'He's on the move,' said Susan. Perry struggled to get up and looked out the window. They weren't in the hotel car park now. In fact, they were in the middle of Inverness. 'Inverness?'

'He's in a taxi,' said Susan. 'I'm following him. I didn't want to wake you up, just in case it was nothing. Maybe he was just going to the shops or whatever.'

'We're coming through Inverness now, though,' said Perry.

'Yes, not sure where we're going, but it looks like we're heading back out of the city, over towards Loch Ness.'

They continued out past the turnoff out to the theatre, continuing on the road and eventually coming up to where the swing bridge was for the canal. Just beyond that, the taxi pulled up in a rather large but very empty car park. Susan drove on past, watching as the man got out of the taxi. She turned around, coming back, and Perry saw Rupert was looking around. And then he walked up towards the golf club.

Susan parked up in the car park, and Perry, with his binoculars, watched Rupert's progress. The golf course was on the edge of Inverness, near the canal, the crematorium just beyond it. There were paths that led up by bushes and trees, and Perry watched as the man disappeared off a path into one of these bushes.

'We're going to have to get out and get close. If he's meeting someone up there, or maybe he's . . . well, maybe he's engaging in something with someone.'

'You can put it better than that,' said Susan. 'I'm not Macleod.'

'Maybe he's making out?'

'Shall I go?'

'It's okay,' said Perry. 'I'll go. You stay here in the car, in case we end up with two people to follow.'

Perry stepped out and felt the cold air. He reached back into the car and pulled out his jacket, wrapping it around him. He needed more than just a suit jacket today, so it was a fleece he had on. Perry ambled up, aware that he probably looked less like a walker than anyone else. But as he got close to the bush that Rupert had disappeared inside, he could hear voices. He was half expecting to hear an illicit sexual rendezvous, but instead there were two men talking in an agitated fashion.

'We have to keep it quiet,' Rupert fizzed. 'We have to make the problem go away. They can't talk.'

'I can take care of it. I can deal with it.'

'You can take care of it? In what way? I mean, this can't come back at all. We have to just shush them.'

'Let me do what I do. I have my methods. Got people I can talk to.'

'I don't know. The press will be all over this.'

'But the press is your problem. Not mine. As far as I see it, there's a business transaction that needs ended. I'm going to end it.'

'Do it properly. Do it quietly. Make the problem go away. All right? Make sure you do that,' said Rupert.

'Of course, I'll make sure of it. You keep it together.'

Perry heard someone start to move and flung himself deeper inside one bush. He watched as the man got out and then walked past him only a few feet away. Perry held his breath. When the man had cleared, Perry pulled out his phone and sent a silenced text over to Susan, telling her to follow the man who had just come past the bush.

Rupert hadn't left yet, and so Perry remained quiet. Eventually, Rupert got up and walked down the path in the same direction as the young man had gone. Perry waited before eventually getting out. He looked down at the car park. Susan wasn't there. Rupert, however, was walking now down towards the canal, across the bridge, and into the town. He appeared to be heading towards the theatre and Perry thought it was strange that he would do this so openly; the press would be there. He'd have to walk through them, but maybe that was the plan, to look normal as he walked.

The man suddenly put a thumb out, and a taxi pulled up alongside him. He jumped in and Perry continued to walk, keeping his face away from the taxi as it went past. He then spotted an unmarked police car coming along and flagged it down quickly.

'All right, Jamesy boy,' said Perry looking in. 'I need you to tail someone for me.'

'I'm meant to be at a conference in five minutes,' protested Jamesy.

'Tell them you're assisting an officer. Won't be a problem.'

The man called it in and headed off after the taxi. But the taxi turned around, headed back across Inverness and ended up back at the hotel. Perry thanked Jamesy and then went inside to the lobby.

He got a cup of coffee and sat in the corner. He could see a few press about, one of whom came up and spoke to him, recognising him as a policeman. Perry quietly told him he was just keeping an eye out in case there was any trouble for the guests. It was reasonable, after all. But he wondered what Susan was up to.

* * *

Susan was a little annoyed at Perry. He'd jumped out of the car; he'd run off. She was the fittest one, the one who could move quickly. She was the one who could handle herself best in a fight. Maybe he just didn't want to be in the car with her. Maybe he didn't want her with him. It had been awkward, and it would get more awkward.

She looked up towards the bush where Perry had jumped in. A man was now walking past it. Then there was a text on her phone.

Follow him.

Just like that. At least Perry has taken his fleece, she thought. She sat in the front seat of the car, pretending to go through her phone as she watched the man get into a car in the car park. He drove off.

Susan gave him a moment before following. He headed out to another car park where he dumped the car and she parked up. Susan watched as he disappeared inside a supermarket.

Susan took the chance to have a quick look over the car. The keys were still in the ignition. She sent a message to the station asking for an identification of the car. It had just been reported stolen. She advised them where it was and then followed the man into the supermarket. She saw him exiting and bought herself a coffee at one of the automated machines before following him back out. He walked on across town, Susan keeping a close eye on him, but from a distance.

On the street in Inverness, he was halted by a young woman. Susan looked at her. What age was she? She was fifteen, seventeen, nineteen maybe. It was hard to tell. What Susan could tell was that wasn't the outfit for a wintry day like this. She practically threw her arms around the man, gave him a kiss, a deep one, and then stood there, waiting. Susan watched as the man's hands went inside his jacket and he slipped out a small packet of something. The woman thanked him again and moved on.

Susan stuck with him, watching from a distance. Perry hadn't messaged. She would not interrupt him in case he was tailing someone. Anyway, she was fine. Out in the open like this, she was happy tailing him. If Perry needed to, he could always look up her phone or it would say where she was.

She watched as the young man then turned into a bar. It wasn't a pleasant-looking one, and she knew it to be full of a rather rough element. She stood outside, wondering what to do. She wasn't dressed in suitable clothing to go in, but the man didn't seem to be coming out.

Susan walked around the rear, wondering if she could get a look inside the bar. There was a window at the back, and she reckoned if she stood on one of the refuse bins, she could see inside. She would be rather evident from the alleyway, though. Susan clambered over to the bin, got on top of it with her knees, and then stood upright before peering in through the window.

The window was small. Inside was dark, but she could see, although she didn't think too many would see her. Her man was sitting at a table. He had a beer in front of him, with no one else sitting near him. His phone was out, sitting on the table, but he wasn't looking at it. It was more like he was waiting for something. He picked it up when it rang, but not to his ear. He put the phone back down again and sat staring ahead. The man picked up the phone as it seemed to ring again. He said something, Susan trying to read his words, but it wasn't easy, and the phone went back down again. He didn't seem to be going anywhere, and had ordered another pint.

'You all right, love?' said a voice behind her.

She turned and saw a man in the alleyway.

'If I find that cheating bastard,' said Susan, 'I'll take his balls off.'

'Whoa, I wouldn't go rushing in there, love. Not a nice place. Not really a place for a woman.'

'Oh, he's not there anyway,' she said. She stepped down and went to walk past the man, but he stopped her for a moment.

'Well, if he's no good, and you want someone else.'

'Get real,' said Susan. She walked off, went round the corner and then came back into the alleyway. The man was gone. But going back up in the bin and standing there watching the whole time wasn't going to cut it. She couldn't go inside either, but she didn't want to leave and get changed in case she missed him coming out. He'd taken a phone call after all.

Susan walked around to the front again. There was a little teashop across the road. It was far enough away that it wouldn't be the best place to watch from, but she could see if he went in and out of the bar. She made her way over and settled down for the day, waiting for the man to come out. Every hour, she'd make sure he was still there, taking a peek from on top of the bin. The way he had sat down, though, was like he was organising something, phoning people.

With a coffee in front of her, she sat looking out the window. She picked up her phone and messaged Perry.

'I'm all right,' she said. 'He's in a bar. I'm going to keep eyes on. You stay on Rupert.'

'Do you want assistance?' asked Perry.

'No,' said Susan. She sat there watching. This was the worst thing she had to do—sit and watch. Trouble was, your mind wandered, and it wandered back to Perry again. She needed out. She needed to go with Emmett. He was a quirky guy, and it would be different. A chance to prove herself on her own. Maybe there'd be less running around, but another string to her bow. And Macleod would make it happen. If she didn't do it now, who knew when she would move?

Hope wouldn't want her to go. She'd got on so well with Hope, but she thought Hope sometimes looked at her like a junior Hope. She was Susan, not Hope, and she was capable of other things. No, she would go with Emmett. Her mind was made up. All she had to do was keep it made up while she was sitting watching, waiting for this guy to make a move. She looked into her coffee cup. It was half empty. It could be a long day.

Chapter 11

Macleod hurried out to his car with his grab bag, desperate to make his plane to Glasgow. Tanya had prepped him, boarding pass already in hand, and by the time he arrived, he could see the boarding image already up on the departures board. He breezed through security, having only the bag over his shoulder, walked straight through and out onto the plane.

Macleod had flown with the regional airline many times and sat back waiting for the departure and the coffee and caramel wafers that would come. The planes were usually of two varieties. Either a pencil jet, which made you think you were flying far, far away, or the rather more sensible and economic ATR. This was the ATR. But despite all the noise inside the cabin, Macleod wasn't bothered.

When his coffee came, he drank it, although he wouldn't have accepted it from a shop. Still, being up in the clouds, it wasn't so easy to nip out, or for the stewardess to bring a proper espresso machine with her. He chewed on the caramel wafer, thinking about the people he was going to meet.

Macleod hadn't spoken to Jameson in years. He'd been back to Glasgow before, the time when he was suspended. There were tough areas down there. He remembered the times back in Glasgow when he felt he had to be a lot stronger than he'd been since he'd come further north. Not that further north didn't have its own troubles.

He hoped his name would get him through the front gate, get him an audience. He couldn't believe that someone like the Jamesons would have shot Morton out there, in the open, in front of the public. It would have been quieter, more discreet, and probably involving a lot more suffering.

The plane landed at Glasgow, and Macleod made his way to pick up the hire car Tanya had secured for him. Then he drove out to the edge of Glasgow, and stopped at a gate that had fenced off a rather small estate. The house up on the hill was grand, but Macleod couldn't look at it with any pleasure. It came from ill-got gains.

He stepped out of his car and walked over towards the gate, but someone was already stalking behind it.

'What do you want?' said a voice.

'I need to talk to Mr Jameson Senior.'

'You're a copper, aren't you? You can piss off.'

'I need to talk to Jameson—Mr Jameson Senior, please.'

'You deaf. I said, "Piss off."'

'Tell him it's Macleod.'

The man behind the gate stopped for a moment, a little unsure.

'Tell him it's Macleod. I don't want to phone him and ask for an audience, to tell him that his goon down here on the gate didn't tell him I was here. Tell him it's Macleod. He'll want to speak to me.'

The man stared at him. 'If this is a windup, if he tells me—'

'Just go do it, son,' said Macleod. That's how they spoke in

Glasgow. That's what he would understand. The younger man picked up his mobile phone and, after a consultation, he told Macleod to wait at the gate. Five minutes later, a car left the house, driving down to the gate. The car pulled up, and an older man got out. Macleod recognised him. He was in his seventies now, had grey hair and walked with a slight limp, but Macleod knew Jameson senior.

A small door in the gate opened, and Jameson stepped through.

'Macleod,' he said. 'The boy said you wanted me.'

'Need to talk to you.'

'You're done though; you're not Glasgow anymore. You're on borrowed time elsewhere, but you're not Glasgow. And I'm done, old man now, both of us. What would you have to talk to me about?'

'Jimmy's just got out, hasn't he?' said Macleod. He'd done his homework.

'Yes,' said Jameson. 'Jimmy's out, why?'

'Has he done anything stupid?'

'I won't let him do anything stupid,' said Jameson. He looked around at the boy on the other side of the gate, and then back to Macleod. 'Let's take this somewhere else.' He pointed over to a path on the opposite side of the road from the house. 'We can walk along there,' he said.

It was a small path, cut through trees, but clearly Jameson didn't want to talk in front of the young man guarding his gate.

'Why are you asking about Jimmy?' he said.

'I've got a dead body on my hands.'

'I thought that's what you did. Nothing unusual in that. It's not my Jimmy. Why would you think it would be my Jimmy?'

'Angus Morton's dead,' said Macleod, 'shot through the head once, theatre in Inverness.'

Jameson eyed him, then almost spat. 'He was a talented actor, I'll give him that, a bloody excellent actor, one of Scotland's best. Had links with our family, but good ones, decent ones, you know, not any coercion or that. He liked to gamble, so I would have him over at illegal card nights. It's good for the boys, you know. All the boys come in, and they're playing cards with Angus Morton. They loved it. I cut ties with him a while back now. A good while back.'

'Why?' asked Macleod.

'Didn't suit,' said Jameson.

'That's rubbish,' said Macleod. 'You wouldn't have cut him because he didn't suit. If he were losing money, you'd have kept him as well. Or you'd have made sure he won some money if you wanted the big star at your nights. I know you, Jameson. You like to show off. He would have been a catch for you. Catch to show the rest of them. But you cut links. Why?'

'I took him to one of the clubs.'

'One of your strip joints?' asked Macleod.

'Gentleman's club. He's in drinking, the girls are putting on a show, nothing illegal, straightforward, you know. We're going to do some cards afterwards, and that, the girls dancing for him, and he turns to me, Macleod. He turns, and you know what he says. He says to me, "Have you got any younger ones?"'

'And what did you say?'

Jameson stopped walking. 'Look Macleod, I know you and I don't see eye to eye. I know you don't agree with what I do. You don't like the places I run, and what goes on, and you may even not like how I conduct my business. How I sort out people who betray me. It's all right. You're a bloody copper.

I'm not. But there's a place where you and I join forces. There's a place where you and I are eye to eye. Girls who work at my club, they're all of age. All of age. I check it. Okay? They don't get in there if they're too young. I check those IDs. We're not like that. You wouldn't want your girl in there. If you have a girl, you wouldn't want her in there young. And you certainly wouldn't want a man like that after.'

'I thought Angus Morton was, well . . . wasn't he a homosexual?' asked Macleod.

'There were a lot of rumours about that, weren't there?' said Jameson. 'I'll tell you something. I took him into the gentlemen's club. His eyes were everywhere. The more I think about it, he was hunting the younger ones. There was a girl there, Cassie. At least, that's what she called herself. I mean, who names somebody Cassie in Scotland? But he kept pointing her out to me. Now Cassie was twenty. But Cassie could look like she was a bit younger. Not that we played that. I wouldn't let her, but you could see him. That's what he wanted. Come to daddy. Any of the girls want to come to daddy? Like I said, you can think of me what you want, but that's not me. I don't do that. I will not have that around me.'

'Of course, you could just be telling me that,' said Macleod.

'Piss off. Don't you even dare to dream of calling me that.' Macleod watched the man's fists roll in.

'You thinking of hitting me for that one?' said Macleod. 'Let's be honest, it'll just be an embarrassment. Two old codgers like us fighting in the dirt. Do more harm to ourselves falling over than we would hitting each other.'

Jameson burst out laughing. 'You're right there. You're right there. We were on TV, one of those documentaries for one of the channels. On the TV documentary, they asked us about different things, and one of the questions was about young girls and the clubs. The one who asked that, she was a female interviewer, and I said to her, "You don't ask that." If she had been a man, I'd have hit him. That's not what I want for my family. I don't mind being seen the other way. We are what we are, Macleod. And yes, I can be brutal with those who look to hurt me, hurt my family. But I don't do that. I think I said to her, I'd happily gut them. And do you know what, Macleod, I would. I would gut them. String them up and, well, the things I would do to them. The things I would take off them.'

'I understand,' said Macleod. And he did. Because inside he was thinking how he could do that too.

'Heard they took a gun to Morton's head and blew it apart? They deserve a medal,' said Jameson. 'You hear me? They deserve a medal. Scum like that. I don't care what he was. Yes, he was an excellent actor. But for me, I regret the time he ever spent with my family. When he asked those things, I came back to the house. I took the photos down. You've never been in my house, Macleod. I have a proper snooker table. It's lovely. But around the walls, I have photographs. People who have been in my clubs or who I've done things with for charity and stuff. I came home, I took the photo of him, and I smashed it, and I burnt it, and I took every bit of him that was in my house, and I got rid of it.'

'Tell your boy to stay out of trouble,' said Macleod. 'You don't need to have a rolling empire. You've got too much stuff now that's, well, it's legitimate.'

'You're giving me advice?' said Jameson. 'I'm out. Right, the only time I get back in now is if somebody comes for the family. Word is, you're out too. I'll give you credit. You were a tough dog. A right tough dog. Spent some time inside because of you. But I don't feel anger towards you. You know that Macleod? I don't. You were doing what you did. You were a test, one of the difficult ones. I almost feel nostalgic about you.'

He turned and walked back to the gates. Macleod strode with him. When they reached, Jameson gave a grin.

'Macleod, don't come back. We've nothing to do with it. But you hang that medal on whoever did it. Okay?'

Macleod watched the older man go through the gate, into the car that was still waiting for Jameson, staring while he was driven back up to the house. The young man who'd originally spoken to Macleod was still at the gate.

'Are you going to stand there? Or are you going to piss off, copper?'

Macleod walked over to the gate. 'You speak to me like that once more, and I'll have this place searched. I'll have so many people around here. And when Mr Jameson asks me what I'm doing, your name will come front and foremost. You will be presented to him. I will leave with my officers. And you will be left talking to him. Let's have an apology.'

The young lad tried to act brave. He almost said the word again, telling Macleod where to go. But Macleod could see the lip wobble. Macleod didn't flinch.

'Sorry then,' said the young man, and he turned and walked, his cheeks burning.

Macleod got back into the car. The trip had been worth it. And he thought about how Jameson had spoken about him. Macleod being such a wonderful opponent. He didn't feel the same. Jameson was scum. He might not have been the scum that messed about with young women, but he was scum. He wrecked lives, took people's money, killed people.

No, Jameson was scum, and Macleod was only too glad to be driving away from him.

Chapter 12

'Teamed up again, Als. Taking my car then.'

Ross looked up from his desk. He'd been searching through more records about Angus Morton, trying to find concrete evidence. He had a name for the gambling syndicate to whom Morton apparently owed money. Slushfunders. Ross knew nothing about them.

'We're a bit early going for the car, aren't we?' said Ross. 'We're going to need to find out who Slushfunders are. I don't think it's wise to harass people with the name of Angus Morton. With his being dead, they will not be keen to talk. It's hard to get—'

'Als, enough. What have you got on them?'

'Slushfunders. The only thing I know is Morton owed money to Slushfunders.'

'Come on then. Down to the car,' said Clarissa.

'What do you mean, down to the car? I'm meant to be staying here. And Slushfunders. It's a slush account. It could be anything. We're in the dark.'

'It's Darryl Slush,' said Clarissa. 'The guy is an idiot. The guy wants to be known.'

'But he doesn't come up on anything, Darryl Slush.'

'No, he doesn't. I'll educate you on the way,' said Clarissa. Ross grabbed his jacket and followed Clarissa's swaying tartan shawl down the stairs towards the car park.

'The boss said you would have an idea about it.'

'Old school, this one. We're doing this old school,' said Clarissa. 'Best way with these people.'

They got into Clarissa's car, Ross putting on the seat belt quickly. The little green sports car then reversed. Clarissa spun the wheel, and she roared out onto the Inverness streets.

'Moving up in the world, Als. Sergeant, Sergeant Ross. You should have stuck with me, could have gone places, could have gone places on the arts team. Pats is doing well. Pats loves being out with me.'

'I'm quite okay where I am,' said Ross. They approached the roundabout, and Ross sat back, waiting for the couple of cars to pass before Clarissa would pull out. His mouth flopped open as she dropped a gear, floored the car, pulled out quickly in front of a vehicle that was racing round the roundabout and off the other side. As she cleared the junction, she turned to look at Ross.

'You all right? You've gone positively white.'

'I forgot how you drive,' he said.

'If you want, I can give Perry or Susan a few lessons, you know?'

'No,' said Ross. 'Where are we going? And how long do I have to be in this car?'

'"How long do I have to be in this car, Inspector?" if you're going to talk like that. You still call Seoras, sir. Haven't you got past that yet?'

'No,' said Ross. 'He deserves it. He's—'

'He deserves it! So why do you call me Clarissa? You don't

call me ma'am. You don't even call me detective inspector.'

'No,' said Ross.

He knew suddenly that Clarissa was staring at him. And continued to stare at him. And then stared some more.

'Would you watch the road?' he said.

'I have driven for how long? I am a bright, bold age, although you may not use those words, and I am still driving. When you're driving at this age, Als, you can talk to me about how to drive.'

'Where are we going?'

'Off to a club. I think that's where he'll be. Daryl Slush came up off the streets. That's why we don't know his real name. We know nothing else because he doesn't go through the normal channels. He doesn't pay tax. He doesn't earn a living except by gambling—gambling and running illegal gambling. However, he does that particularly well. The last I heard, he was involved in a little club near to this fine city that we occupy.

'You never see him because he's always in the back room. He doesn't own any of the premises, but he lives in a lot of them as he moves about. Those who do own them are quite happy for him to be in them because he runs his gambling operation, and he pays a cut to them, and he always keeps the money coming in.'

After a short while, Clarissa pulled up outside what looked like a gentleman's club in Inverness. 'But you said he did gambling.'

'In the back room. Likes places that other people don't come in and out of, places that are secretive and protective because they have to be. He's been in a few working men's clubs as well, places where you have bouncers for good reasons like this.'

'It's not open though,' said Ross. 'Should we watch and wait?'

'I didn't bring this car along to watch and wait. It's a little obvious. Besides,' said Clarissa, 'Daryl's a reactionary. He's used to keeping cards close to his chest unless he has a reason to jump. Let's make him jump.'

'How are you going to do that?'

'You need to make a fuss,' said Clarissa. She picked up her mobile phone and called the station's desk sergeant.

'Detective Inspector Clarissa Urquhart. I'm on a little house call from Macleod. I need to make somebody think you're coming for them. Can I get about three or four of your finest squad cars down to the centre of town? Just along from the strip club. Yes, that one. Jimmy Mellon's. Come in screaming, but go to one of the other buildings along from it. But make it look like you're coming to him. I'll be there, but don't get them to engage with me at all. If they see me, have them warned not to talk to me. I need them not to contact me at all.'

As Clarissa put the phone down, Ross stared at her. 'What are you doing?'

'Told you, he needs a reason to jump. Watch this and follow me.'

They sat there for all of four or five minutes, and then Ross heard the sirens. The cars came screaming around the corner and pulled up right outside the strip club. Clarissa jumped out of her car, ignored the uniformed officers who were getting out, and went straight up to the front door, banging on it loudly.

'Darryl Slush,' she shouted. 'Darryl Slush. We're looking for Darryl Slush.'

There was a commotion inside, and the sirens were still wailing. It took about a minute before the door opened casually.

'You can't come in here,' said a small man. 'You've no need, you've no rights to come in here. I need to see paperwork.'

'I'm sorry?' said Clarissa.

'You can't have a raid. You need the paperwork to conduct a raid. We have done nothing.'

'Is your name Darryl Slush? Or are you referred to as Darryl Slush?'

The man nodded. 'Excellent. I need to talk to you.'

'You can't come in. Not on a raid. Not like this. Where's your paperwork?'

'Why do I need paperwork?' asked Clarissa.

'It's a raid. Look at all the officers.'

Clarissa turned round. 'Wow. Are they here?'

One of the police officers came up. 'Step inside, please, sir. Inside your building. We're just dealing with an incident further down.'

Darryl Slush looked up at Clarissa. 'Do you mind if I step in with you?' she said. 'I don't want to be caught up in whatever's going on here.'

Daryl looked at her, weighing up his options.

'Come on in,' he said. Clarissa stepped through, followed by Ross, and the door was shut behind them. A few lights came on.

'What do you want?' asked Daryl.

'Did you hear about Angus Morton?'

'Dying at the theatre the other night? Heard it was a good show.'

'I was there,' said Clarissa, 'and it wasn't so good a perfor-mance. I take it you know who I am?'

'Of course. But I don't have any artwork. I don't get involved in that. That's not what I do.'

'And what do you do, Daryl?'

'Well, I'm not involved in the arts. And I'm not involved in taking out dead celebrities.'

'This is D.S. Ross. He works for Macleod.' Daryl's face, for a moment, flinched. 'Looking into the death of Angus Morton. And there's been several rumours that he may have owed you money.'

'Whoa, whoa,' said Daryl. 'No, we're not going there.'

'Why not?' asked Clarissa. 'Why are we not going there? Do you know something about it? Do I need to talk to Uniform and ask them to come here and have a search? Do I need to get a warrant?'

'There's nothing here to find, because I didn't do any business with him.'

'That's not the word on the street. That's not the word everywhere,' said Ross.

'I knew him from being an actor. I knew him from—'

'You knew him from playing your card games,' spat Clarissa. 'Somebody like that coming to you, you knew he had money. You'd also be a big star bringing Morton into a game and enticing other people into your game. Other mugs who couldn't really play. And you would get their money and siphon it off. You could keep him there. Not losing too much, keep him in the game. I heard he quite enjoyed a gamble, heard he ran up enormous debts,' said Clarissa. 'I heard he owed you a fortune. Gives you a reason to come after him. I mean, someone who doesn't pay his debt, you need to sort them out, don't you?'

'Never killed anyone over a debt,' said Daryl.

'Well, maybe he was different,' said Clarissa. 'Maybe trying to break a few fingers or threaten him didn't work. Trouble was, if you broke his fingers, we'd come looking, wouldn't we? He's a celebrity. Papers would dig in. Too much heat.'

'I didn't go after him because he's not part of my group. He's not part of anything that I do. Obviously, I don't do any illegal activities.'

'Of course you do illegal activities,' said Clarissa. 'Do you want me to get Macleod down? He sent me off, along with my good friend Als here, to have a word with you. You see, Macleod said, "It's probably not Daryl." I said, "Well, I think I should check that out. Make it known for sure." Because then, if there's any doubt, we'll come in fully. Make it big. A lot of press around watching us do it as well. I mean, club owners will not like that, will they?

'I said I could get there in quiet, you know. And if Daryl's been a good citizen, we can just let him go. We can just, you know, not bother him in his lawful daily business. Obviously, the people he works with will be quite happy that there wasn't a lot of fuss and a lot of—'

'Okay. Okay,' said Daryl.

'What's the deal with Angus Morton?' asked Clarissa. 'I want everything.'

'The man played okay. The man couldn't get enough of cards. He liked to gamble. He liked the thrill, I think. But he wasn't a card player. He wasn't good.'

'Novice level or what?'

'Absolute idiot. I taught him some very basic stuff, just so he wouldn't get blown away by some of the other people. But you had to keep him on tables that had other people who were pretty rubbish too. And the money would come in from them. I'd put a ringer in who would get lucky and win. Different one each time, and gradually we siphoned their money off. But I made sure Angus didn't get too deep in debt, and then, in truth, I got greedy. And he kept going on and on. He ended up in debt. Enormous debt.'

'So what? You just sent somebody to sort him. I mean, that's your normal thing, isn't it? Send a few heavies round, a few questions.'

'No. No,' said Daryl. 'The man's too much of a public figure. He's too high-level. The last thing I needed was any comeback from it. Somebody shot him. You've seen the papers. It's everywhere. That's not how I operate. I'm quiet, in the back. I'm away from everything. And let's be honest, I'm dealing with people who can afford to lose money. I'm not the lottery. I'm not taking money off people who can ill afford it, wishing on a prayer. My money comes from people in big business who want the thrill of being clandestine. I'm not really doing any harm.'

'Spare me the talk,' said Clarissa. 'Just tell me about Angus Morton.'

'Nothing to tell. He owed me money, but I took so much money off the others who came in to sit with him, I just wrote it off. It wasn't worth it. It really wasn't worth it.'

'Did he go to any other tables? Anything run by anybody else?'

'He did. A couple. But they didn't know how to handle him. They didn't know how to coax him along. And by that point, he was running out of money. It wasn't worth it. You have to play people right; you don't just rip them apart,' said Daryl. 'He was an excellent investment, worth my time, worth what I did to get him involved. But I bled him dry, bled the celebrity status dry. I took him as an asset that paid, even though he owed money personally. What I got from him far outstripped what he owed me, so he didn't really owe me it.'

'And everyone else involved shares your generous point of view?' asked Clarissa.

'I have heard nothing of a kill order. I've heard nothing of anybody wanting to pressurise him from the money point of view. No, he's a national treasure. You stay away. Can I ask you to leave now, in case the people that own this place show up?'

'I find out the truth is different, if I find you've told me a pile of lies,' said Clarissa, 'I won't need a load of uniform coming in here with me. Instead, I will come in here and tear you apart. I will make it my personal ambition and mission in life to remove you from all criminal activity.'

'In my business, I have to read people,' said Daryl. 'I'm telling you what I'm telling you because you won't come back. Because it's good, the information I've given you. And because you don't really care about the people I took the money from. I don't destroy people. They need to make more money and come back with it for me to take it off them again. I make them happy in some ways.'

'Stop,' said Clarissa. 'Thank you for your cooperation. Next time, just open the door before we get blue lights.'

Clarissa walked out with Ross in tow, and they heard the door slam behind them.

'There you go. Didn't take long, did it?' said Clarissa.

They looked down the road and saw a police car with two uniformed officers sitting in it, almost sticking a thumbs-up to Clarissa, who was laughing loudly.

'Sometimes, Als, you've got to learn how to play people. Gets things done a lot quicker. Of course, don't let them catch you doing it. And it gives the troops a laugh. Gets them on your side too. Let's get you back to the office.'

'Plenty of time,' said Ross. 'We've got plenty of time. Just take it easy on the speed.'

'Safest drive you'll ever find, this side of Glasgow,' said Clarissa. Ross was not looking forward to the next ten minutes.

Chapter 13

Eric Patterson had received a phone call from Hope advising him to check out some details for a case Macleod and she were working on. It would give him a chance away from Clarissa because he seemed to follow her around. His relationship with Clarissa was quite love-hate in a lot of ways.

She was full of drive, excitement and did indeed have a unique way of getting to the bottom of things. But she was also outrageous, and not always in a good way, not always in a pleasant way. 'Pats,' as she called him—the only person in the station who called him 'Pats'—was not a name he enjoyed. But he felt he was getting his own back on her now.

He'd worked with her enough to throw in the odd prompt. To toss in a rebuke. As long as he landed it accurately. As long as it pointed out something about her that wasn't good, she seemed to take it. He found it hard to feel bad about Clarissa, anyway, for the woman had saved his life. As he adjusted the cravat around his neck, which hid the scar from the slash across his throat, he remembered fondly how she'd fought to save his life.

Still, it was good to get away on his own occasionally. The

art world had been good to him. He'd learnt a lot. But this was back to the detective work he'd done before.

Hope had said there had been a father who had claimed that he would kill Angus Morton because he was having an affair with his young son. The report had been in the paper, and Patterson had spent the first half hour of the morning finding that report, the man's name, and then running down where he lived. He was north of Inverness, and Patterson got into the car and drove happily up the A9 before pulling off into one of the smaller villages.

It took a mere five minutes for him to find the house. After he parked, Patterson rapped on the door. A man approached before opening it. He was still in his dressing gown and had a sweep of black hair that had thinned so much you could see the baldness on top of his head.

'Hello, sir. My name is Detective Constable Eric Patterson. I'd like to ask you some questions about Angus Morton and a certain newspaper article that you were quoted in, in which it was alleged that you'd like to kill him?'

The man quickly looked past Patterson, both ways. 'Come in, come in,' he said. Patterson stepped in, and the man closed the door, almost catching the constable. 'Come into the living room,' he said. The man raced on ahead, closing the blinds of the living room before offering Patterson a seat.

'Have you been having some trouble?' asked Patterson.

'No. No, I haven't. I wish I'd never done that bloody article.'

'I take it you know that Mr Morton is dead.'

'How could I not be aware Mr Morton was dead?' said the man, pointing at a paper.

'Before I go any further,' said Patterson, 'can I just confirm that you are Mr Lawrence Tillman.'

'Yes, I'm Lawrence Tillman. My son, Andrew Tillman, isn't here anymore. Andrew went off to university.'

'And was Andrew having some sort of affair? Was he approached at all by Mr Morton?'

'No. The whole thing was got up by the press. The pressman came round and said he would offer me a load of money if I would mention the idea that Andrew might be having an affair.'

'With all due respect,' said Patterson, 'why on earth would you put your son through that?'

'Andrew wouldn't have minded. Andrew is of that persuasion. So, his friends knew. It wasn't the case that he was being outed. He also wanted to go to university. I couldn't afford it. Andrew also had a connection with Andrew Morton. He'd been in the theatre, he'd done some backstage work, and he'd met the man. Andrew had gone into his dressing room, but he'd gone in with several other people. Nothing happened, but the pressman said they could cut the other people being there. They could muddy the waters, and they could run a line from it.'

'And you went along with this.'

'Yes, I wanted the money. I told him various facts about Andrew being there, and then I said, if I'd found out that Morton had ever laid a finger on my boy, I would kill him. Well, I knew for a fact that Morton hadn't laid a finger on my boy, and, therefore, I would not kill him. But then they twisted that statement, and it came out that there were deep rumours of an affair and all this stuff. My Andrew found it quite funny, and we got paid, and he got to university. His friends all knew it was a laugh too. That's why the story ran nowhere,' said the man. 'Trouble is now, of course, he's dead and people bring stuff up. I thought at first you were going to be one of the news people, coming back. I want nothing to do with it this time, you know?'

'How old was your boy at that point?'

'Andrew was twenty. He'd wanted to go to university for a couple of years, but we couldn't afford it. He was trying to work towards it, but—'

'Doesn't Scotland pay for those to go to university? I thought you could go to a Scottish university easily.'

'We're not from here. We had moved up; he was past the school age. He couldn't get the grant; therefore, we'd have to pay, effectively.'

'Okay,' said Patterson. 'So, you lied, you took some money, and they cooked up the story. That's it.'

'Basically.'

'Who was the pressman who helped you do this?'

'It was a Fred Heibel,' said Tillman.

'I remember him, Fred Heibel. He worked for the Inverness Freeman.'

'That paper no longer exists. And no wonder—it was cooking up stories. It was part of the reason. He was trying to sell more and more. His editor told him just to get whatever, and if they sold enough, they would cover the cost of paying me off.'

'What did they give you?' asked Patterson.

'Ten grand.'

'And that would cover the fees?'

'Got us in. We had some savings, but we couldn't cover it all. Anyway, Andrew went. He's working now. He's quite happy.'

'Well, I will not pursue any further what you're saying. I can't, frankly, be bothered,' said Patterson. 'You made up a story, so you got paid for it. I don't like it, but hey. I will check with the pressman just to make sure it's all legitimate, but, otherwise, I won't be back. And probably best you keep out of the limelight. Papers will go hell-for-leather about anything to do with Angus Morton.'

'I realise that.'

'Don't worry about them coming because of my visit either. I'm not directly attached to the team that is looking into Mr Morton's demise. Nobody's bothered about where I'm going today.'

'Good,' said the man. 'I hope so.'

'I would warn your boy, though, just in case anything comes. People may want to speak to him.'

Patterson left the house and made his way back towards Inverness. He remembered the scandal-ridden paper, the *Inverness Freeman*. It wasn't a good rag. It wasn't even a gutter rag. But he would need to talk to Fred Hybel. Going back to the office, Patterson searched and found that Fred Hybel was now living out on a council estate.

The day was still reasonably pleasant as Patterson made his way over. He parked the car, locked it, and then made for a small house. He rapped on the door and heard a grumble from the back. Eventually, the door opened, and the man standing there was wheezing.

'What the bloody hell do you want? I take ages to get to the door these days. It takes me so long. And what do you want?'

'I'm a detective, Constable Eric Patterson. I need to talk to you. Are you Fred Hybel?'

'Yeah, Fred Hybel. What's it got to do with? Oh,' he said. 'Is this Morton?'

'Yes, it is, sir. I need to have a chat with you.'

Hybel waved at him, and Patterson walked into a house that stunk of smoke. When he got to the living room, Patterson could see a cigarette still burning. What he found bizarre was that as the man sat down, he reached over for an oxygen mask, took a deep breath from it, and then grabbed his cigarette again. *Not ours to judge*, thought Patterson.

'I've just been to visit a Lawrence Tillman who you ran a story with about Angus Morton back in the day. Apparently, Andrew Tillman, Lawrence's son, had some sort of affair, an attachment to Mr Morton, and Lawrence said he would kill him.'

Fred took a deep puff of cigarette. 'That was . . .' He stopped and coughed loudly. Then began again. 'That was . . . well, paper was on its knees. Needed something. Needed something to generate sales. The editor had a superb idea that Angus Morton would be great for it. And to be honest, Morton was worth it. He said, well . . . he said he'd do it for the publicity.'

'Hang on a minute,' said Patterson, 'Morton wanted a story run about him where he was said to be a homosexual and said to be having an affair with a young lad?'

'The boy was twenty. It was a time when coming out was okay. It was no longer illegal to be homosexual, so he couldn't get done for it. And he wanted it to be out there without having to come out and say it.'

'Why?' asked Patterson.

'All publicity's good publicity. It worked for us. We ran the story. Mr Tillman was absolutely delighted to take our money. Said his lad needed to get to university.'

Fred stopped for a moment. Then he began coughing. Patterson sat for a minute while the man coughed, brought up some phlegm into a dirty old handkerchief, before continuing again.

'Nobody got hurt. Nobody. It's long gone. Like I said, it worked for Morton. He wanted it to be put out there.'

'Why?' asked Patterson. 'What else did he need to cover up? What else could that story do for him? You wouldn't want to be known as gay, would you, at that time?'

'It's what he wanted.'

'But it was when it still would have been a shock. Still, it would have been headline news. Still would have—.'

'You couldn't touch Morton. They could have said he was Darth Vader and people would still have loved him.'

'So, there was nothing in it. Nothing to the story.'

'Nothing at all. You were paid to do it. Minor scandal. That's it.'

'You'd be prepared to swear to that.'

'I have little reputation. I was a hack. I'm still a hack. In fact, I'm not even working anymore. And I'm a dying hack. Cancer. So, you'd better come and get your statements soon.'

Fred looked up. 'He had some links to some nasty people down in Glasgow. Nothing could ever be attributed to him. I know they dropped him quickly. We had run our story not long after that, I think. Anyway, we weren't the sort of paper to go down to Glasgow and run stories about hoodlums. Not hoodlums who could come and break your arms for talking about them. We ran stuff that wasn't true. Fancy fun. Bus on a moon job, you know.'

The man coughed again. 'I don't know anybody who would want to kill him. Too famous to be killed at the end of the day. National treasure. Once you get that status, there are a lot of things you can cover up. A lot of things to cover up and reasons to do it. But I'm sorry, I don't know what he's covering up for if he did.'

The man coughed. Patterson said he'd make his own way to the door. Outside, he got into the car, thought for a moment. It was all a bit strange. But it made sense. It made sense from everybody else's point of view. Mr Tillman got money. His son was already known to be gay, so there was no shock to the family. No shock to his friends. It went into a rag that nobody really believed. They may have sold more papers. And for some reason, Angus Morton wanted it, was happy to go along with it, and was delighted with it.

That bit was the mystery. What was the benefit to Angus Morton other than cheap publicity? Publicity that, well, not that great, was it? Even if it were free. Patterson sighed. He didn't know the entire case. Didn't know everything that was being looked into. He'd go back, and he'd give his report to Hope or Macleod. And then it was back to see Clarissa. There were a couple of art thefts he had to look into, and the day was getting on. He smiled and started the car. At least he'd have a safe journey back to the base.

Chapter 14

Hope, in some ways, felt a little out of sorts. She was back as Macleod's wingman, and rather than running the investigation as she'd got used to recently, she was now at his beck and call. Or rather, she had to follow orders. Hers was to look after things while Macleod disappeared down to Glasgow.

She had contacted Frances Jollye to find out that the director would meet with the actors and the stage crew to discuss what would happen in the future. As often happens with these things, once the initial shock had died down, the business had to work out how to continue. And the business technically had a play to put on in Aberdeen in two weeks' time.

The Inverness run would probably be cancelled completely. Could they get someone in quick enough? If they did, they could start rehearsing soon. They'd been running without stand-ins, which had been a gamble, but nobody expected the lead actor to die. Hope arrived at the council offices along from the theatre where the troupe had gathered. There was a police presence around them because the reporters would have been all over them. Hope flashed her ID at two constables, who clearly knew her anyway, and entered the room to see the troupe sitting down in a sort of circle.

'Don't bother about me,' said Hope. 'Please go on, discuss what you need to. I'm just here to find out what's going to happen so I can make sure there are arrangements to keep the press off your backs and also so we can interview you if needs be.'

'Okay,' said Frances.

Despite saying not to bother with her, many of the actors kept looking over at Hope as Frances began talking about Aberdeen.

'We're due to start there within two weeks. If we can get somebody on board quickly, we can get rehearsals and get going.'

'It'll have to be a pro then,' said Sandra. 'It'll also have to be a big fish. If you get a big fish, the crowds will come out. If you get somebody who doesn't look close to Angus, well then, it's not worth doing.'

'It's not really your decision, that one,' said Frances. 'The money says that we need to keep going.'

'Well then the money,' said Alistair, 'as Sandra says, needs to provide a big fish.'

'You're all contracted in at the moment,' said Frances. 'Now obviously, if you feel you can't continue, we can look at that.'

'I take it you're speaking to the others,' said Sandra. 'You need me. I'm a big enough name to be staying on the board. You can lose the rest of this lot and fill them with someone else.'

'Well, thanks,' said Helen.

'Won't be a problem,' said Sandra. 'Just because you've got some boobs to flash doesn't mean they can't replace you with somebody else and her boobs.'

'I'm here for my acting ability. They said that.'

Sandra waved her hand in the air. 'Of course you are, love. Bit of TV coverage you had done you proud.'

Rupert looked nervous. 'Wouldn't it be better just to close and go on? Start something different.'

'Not how the business works, love,' said Alistair. 'Gotta make the money back. Gotta make money. The money isn't there . . . we don't have jobs. We're actors. We go with the money. You might get all sentimental about this, but this is a business. You're in the business of acting, not in the drama workshops.'

'You've done all right, Rupert,' said Frances. 'I won't lie to you. We can get somebody to take over your part if you want to drop out, but if you need to stay with us, the job's yours. I'm not looking to bring in someone else to pick up all those extra parts you do. You do them fine.'

'High praise indeed,' Sandra said.

'Fine; look,' said Frances, 'I'm running with a small crew here. When we run this small crew, it's best to have people who know each other and not swap people in and out. If we were going with a new lead, I'd want at least six weeks to bed them in, to go through rehearsals. We haven't got that. So yes, we'll need to get somebody good and get on with it. As much as you all don't love each other, you at least know how to work together, and we'll keep that going. We swap three or four people in, it just doesn't work. I need a lot more rehearsal time. So, are you on board?'

'A professional, of course. I'll be here, Frances,' said Sandra.

'Me too,' said Alistair.

'Well, I need to work,' said Rupert. 'And if there's nothing else lined up—'

'That's it,' said Alistair, 'you're getting the idea now, commitment to the cause, commitment to the money.'

'If you need me,' said Helen, 'I think I've already mentioned that.'

'Oh, right,' said Frances. 'I will get on to it. I will get on to the powers that be. We will get ourselves a lead actor. In the meantime, do nothing silly. Talk little to the press. Keep the scandals out.'

'Scandal has already broken. They shot him,' said Sandra.

Listening to them, Hope wondered exactly what was going on. Could the death of Angus Morton actually have been beneficial? Would more people come out? That being said, the reviews were rave. It was doing well. Killing him might burst that bubble. The show was now a guaranteed success, so why would you do it? No, it didn't seem sensible.

Rupert is obviously vulnerable, though, thought Hope. He'd been tracked by Perry and Susan, and now there was this other man sitting around. Perry had gone to get some sleep while Susan continued to watch him and would look to take over later. Rupert was clearly hiding something, but maybe there was a reason to stay within the troupe. Maybe that was a reason to move on to Aberdeen. Could stories go with them? Would he be able to control it better though, going to Aberdeen?

Hope looked at Helen. It was harsh to call her the actress with the boobs. She was a genuine mess on the night, but then again, these were actors. They knew how to portray, knew how to stir your emotions. You'd have to be careful, were they even acting here as they discussed with each other? It was one of those things that churned round your head, and you went round and round in circles never really getting to a point of understanding. Never to a point where you were comfortable with what you thought about them.

Hope's phone vibrated. She picked it up. Jona was requesting her presence at the theatre. Hope excused herself and walked the short distance over to the theatre, where she was met by Jona.

'We've done most of what we need to do,' said Jona. 'I tried calling the boss but he's away, still down in Glasgow.'

'Well, you've got me. What have you found?'

'Can't find a trace of anyone back here who we don't know about. Our actors and our stage crew all gave fingerprints and hair and, of course, they're all over here. We can find their fingerprints, their hair. I asked for the fingerprints and hair samples from those who work here in the theatre, and they were only too ready to give them. I have got nothing here, be it a fingerprint or be it a hair, that I don't know who it is.'

'So, what are you saying?' I asked Hope.

'I'm saying that as far as I can work out, I have got no one backstage who shouldn't have been. A separate gunman. Somebody who hid out. I can't find anyone like that. Not a fingerprint or DNA trail.'

'So you're saying there wasn't a shooter; there wasn't a separate person.'

'I'm saying it's unlikely. It doesn't mean it wasn't possible. Finding out what's going on isn't always a simple science. They may have left no traces. They may have been that good.'

'But?' said Hope.

'It's surprising. To find no evidence of someone back here, if someone had been here, is surprising. Not unheard of, but surprising. However, I have found something else.'

Jona took Hope backstage into the wings. 'Here,' said Jona, 'look, this is the area the shots have come from.' Everywhere was dark. The lights of the stage not filtering through because of black draped curtains, barriers, to prevent people seeing into the wings.

'Now the shot was clear. It doesn't clip any of these curtains, these drapes. These drapes will hide people, but you still have to shoot through them if you're going to hit someone. If you come onto the stage for a minute, you'll see that this is where Angus was shot. That's where he was standing.' She pointed down to the X on the floor.

'What's that?' asked Hope.

'That's a stage marking. When they've got props on the move, or when there are specific places, you need to stand for certain scenes, they mark the stage. You can't see it from the audience, but you can see it as an actor.'

'Okay,' said Hope. 'So, he was standing there.'

'Yes. And over there's where Helen was standing. You see that mark? So, the shot's coming along here,' said Jona, pointing back to the wings, and marched over. 'And when it comes in, it's coming from around this area.' Now standing in the wings, Jona pointed down to the floor. 'Now look here.'

'There are some holes in the floor. Plastic inserts,' said Hope.

'Yes, there are. Are they meant to be there? They are unusual?'

'You're telling me,' said Jona. 'I'll tell you something though. Look at the shape. Tripod,' she said.

'A tripod, that's nice and stable,' said Hope.

'These particular inserts, they are the outer sleeve of a fixing. They will hold something to the floor. They're also quick release.'

'Are you saying something could have been inserted here? Some sort of framework?'

'Certainly, you could put a frame here, and you could get rid of it quickly,' said Jona.

'The frame though. What would the frame be? If you put a gun on it, what size of frame would you need?'

'Well, I said that we thought the shooter was possibly kneeling down because of the angle of the bullet. Therefore, it's going to be about this high.' Jona indicated the frame would be about the hip height of Hope.

'So, they would have to grab the frame and the gun and get out of here. We didn't see anybody leave, never mind the frame.'

'No, but I'll tell you something. With these fixings here, you could reach down and get them out if you had thirty seconds, maybe even get underneath and do them.'

'And that would leave some holes,' said Hope.

'It would. It would leave some holes.'

'Were the holes there originally?' asked Hope.

'These holes have been here, according to the house manager, for a couple of years now.'

'So somebody could have known they would have been here; somebody could have known that this would be the opportunity to fix something onto them.'

'The inserts are not part of what should be here; it should be these three holes. It was done for a production several years ago in which none of the crew were involved.'

'If you put a gun on here though,' asked Hope, 'how does that work?'

'Automated weapon. If you had a weapon there and you had it set up correctly, it could shoot.'

'But it can't aim, can it?'

'Well, strictly you can get guns you can be in touch with and small cameras on so you can see. That sounds overly complicated to me. If you know where everybody's going to be at a certain point, you could set your gun up to fire there.'

'And if nobody's about, if nobody's near it, it'll work fine. If nobody is in that area, all you've got to do is sneak in quickly, attach it, and then get rid of it.'

'Exactly. I wonder if Clarissa saw it,' said Jona.

'She would have said. She'd have gone right there. Look, if you're going to operate it, you need to know he's going to be in the right position,' surmised Hope. 'Is there a sensor pad or something there?'

'No, there's nothing else on the stage. It would have to be activated by a person. Either that, or you have to be sending a signal out from the gun that then gets returned to say something's in the correct place. The trouble with that is people walk across the stage beforehand. You could set it off early.'

'So, somebody has to activate it,' said Hope

'This is all still supposition. We don't know what was there. I'm just saying that this is a possibility. The evidence says there isn't an extra person. We have found nothing to say there's an extra person there with a gun shooting. Therefore, the bullet has to arrive from somewhere. I'm just saying this is an option,' said Jona.

'An automated weapon, predetermined that Angus Morton would be there. Well, you know that because that's what he does. You'd also have to make that marking. You know he's going to be in exactly that position. At that point, he's also, I believe, looking over at Helen. He's facing the right way, motionless. He's not on the move because he's having a gun pointed at him in the story,' said Jona.

'It makes sense. He stands in place, frozen, and he has to be in that place because he's centre stage. It's part of the act. They have a point at which they know he's going to be there. They'll know roughly where his head is, and they'll take a pot shot and if it misses,' said Hope, 'it's going to bury itself up there and nobody will be any of the wiser because Angus will have been thrown backwards. He'll just be standing there, and you think that the gun's gone off.'

'It's not watertight,' said Jona, 'but it's certainly a possibility.'

'And it's one that Seoras is going to want to know about. Thank you, Jona,' said Hope, 'you might be on the move to solving this.'

Chapter 15

Macleod hung his coat up inside his office. He picked up the phone and placed a quick call to his own house.

'Hello?'

'Jane,' said Macleod. 'How are you?'

'I'm fine. Clarissa dropped by.'

'I thought she might. She's been doing a bit of work for me, but she's not really on this case.'

'Okay. I have had no bother. No press or that.'

'That's because they're used to the idea that they get nothing out of me. So, they never come fishing.'

'Have you had a busy day?' asked Jane.

'Been to Glasgow and back today. Just about to meet with the team. Hopefully, I might get home for a bit of sleep tonight. If not, I'll get a few hours in here. One good thing about this office, there's a sofa in the corner. It's good to get to sleep on.'

'Let me know. I'll come in.'

'What? And have the scandal of me bringing women into my office through the night.'

'You're leaving soon. Who cares?' said Jane. Macleod laughed. She was fun like that.

'Do you think you're going to clear it up soon? Is it going to be a long case? Clarissa said you were running it.'

'I am, and you know why. Protecting Hope with it. I'm hoping it will not be a long one, but you can never really tell. We're making headway. At least I think we are.'

'Don't let it be a millstone. You have to walk away at some point. At some point, you'll have to hand it over if it keeps going. We're not putting off our adventure for a year.'

'I don't think I'd last a year,' said Seoras, suddenly going quiet.

'Seoras, you all right?'

'I was talking to a man today. A man who's not nice. I was talking about something another man did with very young women, not pleasurable things. This other nasty man, he said that he would have gutted him for it. I found myself not disagreeing. I've always looked to the law, looked to the legal way of doing things. Now I've seen that it doesn't always work, and when you get something as as gross as this, well I find myself agreeing with things I never would have agreed with. Not that I would do it myself.

'I need out, Jane. It's time to go. I think we both know that!'

'And you are nearly out. One last push. One last push, Seoras. Focus. Get it done. And get home.'

'Will do. I'll call if I can. Love you.'

'That's my man. I'll see you soon.'

Macleod put the phone down. When he did, he received a call from downstairs, Hope advising him that the rest of the team were there. Macleod made his way down to Hope's office and saw them around the little table to the side. It was the one he'd sat with them at so often when this was his office.

'So, what do we know?' asked Macleod.

'Well,' said Hope, 'we might be looking for an automated gun. We've got an idea of a stand that was fixed in place with quick fixings, then taken away along with the gun.'

'Does that mean it's still there?' asked Macleod.

'Well, it wasn't there,' said Hope.

'Is it hidden?'

'How do you hide a stand like that? This thing was up to my hip. Jona was indicating. it's a tripod; there to give stability, so it's not thin. I mean, you're talking a good foot or two apart, some of these poles that were going into the floorboards.'

'But you just don't walk in with a stand,' said Macleod. 'It would have to have been broken down. It would have to have been hidden to be brought in. If you can do that, you can do it the other way.'

'That's right,' said Perry.

Macleod looked around him suddenly. 'Where's Susan?'

'She's still on that stakeout,' said Perry. 'I'm going to relieve her as soon as I'm done here. I talked with her, and she said it would be better if I came in and did this. Then she can get off to bed as soon as I take over. She hasn't slept yet.'

'Well, no,' said Macleod. 'Some of the rest of us haven't either.'

'I can look into tripods for guns,' said Ross.

'Yes,' said Hope. 'Look into it.'

'Look into how to build one of these, but also,' said Macleod, 'look into who can build one of these. Look at the troupe. Who's got the ability? Who's got the skills to make one? That's the first port of call. If nobody has, then we look to who would have the knowledge to find someone who can build one.'

'Props people might be a good place to start,' said Ross.

'What else have we got?' asked Macleod.

'Clarissa did us wonders,' said Hope. 'Angus Morton was in debt, but our gambling fraternity had made so much money out of him they just left him alone. So, he was an asset that was used up and was no longer viable. More hassle to kill him; more hassle to get rid of him given how public a figure he was than it was worth.'

'And Jameson, who I visited in Glasgow, head of the criminal family Morton had connections to, he said something very similar,' said Macleod. 'But he also cut ties with him because Angus Morton at one of Jameson's strip clubs, asked if there were any younger women. He was looking for girls, underage. Jameson wouldn't stand for that. The nasty bugger he is, it's not something he goes for. Said he wanted to gut him.'

'Does that mean Jameson could have killed him?'

'No,' said Macleod. 'Doesn't mean he wouldn't assist some-body who was doing it, but not himself directly. Definitely not directly. He wouldn't have done it like this if he had done it directly, anyway. Quieter, he'd be much cleaner, in a sense.'

'Well, it's pretty clean,' said Hope. 'We haven't found out who's doing it.'

'I see a man,' said Macleod, 'covering up for some sort of addiction or hunger. Possibly young women. He's in the public spotlight. He's going to need money if he's going to procure, that sort of thing. Maybe that's where the gambling comes from.'

'Looking at his travels over the last number of years, he's gone out to the Far East several times,' said Ross. 'Flights to Bangkok, places around there. He's also flown to a lot of other places that normal tourists go to as well. And of course, you can go to these places and not be involved in anything like that. But if that's his tastes, he's certainly going to places that would cater for that.'

'So he may have angry victims, fathers, brothers,' said Macleod.

'Patterson reported in earlier,' said Hope. 'Eric said that there wasn't anything to the newspaper report, saying he was into boys.'

'In fact,' said Macleod, 'Patterson said it was a setup job, didn't he?'

'A setup job?' said Perry. 'Maybe he's deflecting from the girls. That's the thing, isn't it? If you've been labelled as a homosexual, nobody's going to look twice if you're around young women. Makes sense. They know it's not your cup of tea. Then there's no problem standing around them, no problem being seen with them, no problem with them visiting you. Best deflection going!'

'So, do we reckon he's promoting a taste that he isn't involved in hiding one that he is?' asked Macleod.

'Well, that makes sense,' said Hope. 'So, what are we looking at then? Brothers? Family members? Angry victims? We need to find someone who's got a connection to that sort of life. Maybe someone who's had someone abused, someone who's been used, been in it themselves. A campaigner. Something like that would certainly give a motive to kill him.'

'Still, nobody's claimed it. Nobody's come forward and said,' said Perry.

'No, they haven't,' said Macleod. 'So that means we're dealing with someone who's dealing with personal grief, personal injury, possibly. They don't care about his being held up under the light.'

'They just want him dead, but they're inventive enough,' said Perry. 'They're inventive enough to find a way of doing it that shows that somebody came in and killed him because they want to get away with it. He's been shot from the wings in a place there nobody is, nobody can see, and then the mysterious gunman gets out.'

'But they're not aware,' said Hope, 'of all the door people.'

'It's usual house people though, isn't it in a theatre?' asked Macleod. 'Protecting the backstage.'

'To a point,' said Hope, 'but this theatre had put it on overload because it was Angus Morton.'

'So, their plan, if they hadn't stuffed up so much, might have worked? The unknown gunman disappearing.'

'Also, if you hadn't got up on stage, they could have got in and removed those plastic inserts that were in the floorboards,' said Hope. 'Then you've got three holes. There's no sign anything's been there. We're not looking for an automated weapon. We're looking for a gunman.'

'It's really clever, isn't it?' said Macleod.

'Well planned,' said Ross. 'Someone with an analytical mind, someone used to solving problems, someone used to seeing . . .' And then he stopped.

'Used to what, Ross?' asked Macleod.

'Building the illusion.'

'Well, we're in the theatre,' said Perry. 'I'm afraid illusions come as second nature.'

Macleod looked around them. They were getting somewhere, but there was still a long way to go.

Hope's phone rang, and she walked over to answer it. From the tone of her voice, Macleod knew it was something serious. She turned back.

'That was Susan. Our young man's on the move. She's following him in a car, but she's heading on to the Lamas estate.'

'She doesn't want to be there on her own,' said Perry. 'It's getting dark out.'

'Well, she has asked for backup.'

'Hope, take Perry and Ross to assist. That guy's key at the moment. We need to make sure he doesn't get away, and if he's meeting someone, we need to make sure we know about it.'

'Will do,' said Hope, turning and grabbing her jacket off the nearby hangar. 'Let's go guys,' she said.

Ross was up and running out to his computer, to get his own jacket, while Perry shambled up. Macleod, however, stayed in the office while the team left. The lights were on in the office, and he stood behind Hope's desk. From the window he could see their car as it left, but he stood looking.

This had been his view, and although it was now dark, he could tell you which lights belonged to which streets as they went off into the distance. He'd stood there so many times. Upstairs wasn't the same; it truly wasn't. He also would have raced out the door in the past. He was getting slower and wasn't as fit as he had been. Macleod wasn't as good as he had been at following people, staying in the shadows, remaining aloof and then finding them, trapping them.

Macleod wondered if he'd get to bed that night. That was different too. He never wondered if he would get to bed on a case. He knew he really needed to go to bed. But he would never wonder. Ask the question. You just did what you had to do. But right now, he wanted to get back to bed. Wanted to curl up and feel Jane beside him. He wanted to have a lie-in tomorrow because his shoulders were sore, his bones were aching. He wanted out. A couple of years ago, he couldn't have seen this. He couldn't have known that he would want to go. It was time.

He looked over at Hope's whiteboard. It still had the stage on it, the places marked. They'd put an X on the floor, he had walked to the X, he stood, and somebody had fired the gun, remotely, with some sort of mechanism. But they knew Angus Morton would be there. The shot, the trajectory, didn't endanger the public.

This was very specific, but it was also amateur. A pro never would have taken that shot. He'd have waited until he got outside the theatre, shot him in an alleyway, shot him in a bar, shot him somewhere. And let's face it, the man went places that were illicit. That was clear from his lifestyle. Macleod had found that out without a lot of difficulty. A pro would have found that out too. A pro would have watched him.

It was an amateur killing, but an amateur killing with a lot of planning and a lot of ability. Who activated the gun and how? Macleod ran through that night. Ran through getting up on the stage. Thinking about looking to the wings, he never saw a gun. He never saw the tripod. Was it gone by that point? Where had it gone? What did they do with it? It must be there somewhere, and if they could find it, maybe they could trace who built it.

Then things unravel. You might have to go back and have a look again. Have a look at the theatre. Think about where you could put things, but not right now. Right now, he'd wait to see what his team would say. Maybe they'd be talking to someone. Maybe they'd be bringing Rupert in. This was a weird connection. What was it about?

He'd have to wait. And so, Macleod did wait. He made himself a coffee at the machine inside the large office outside, brought it in and stood looking out the window. Coffee in hand, he waited for his phone to vibrate. Waiting for a message to say they'd done what they needed to do. And as he looked out, he thought this would be one thing he'd miss, the view. Not the job, but the view from the best office in the world.

Chapter 16

Susan Cunningham stood on the street corner watching the man cross the road. She was wearing jeans and a long leather jacket. It was something she'd done recently, trying to differentiate herself from Hope. They dressed in similar types of clothes, but Susan wanted to be different. Hope's jackets were never this long at three-quarter length. Susan might wear them from now on. However, she had to focus.

The street they were on was not a nice one. Some houses were boarded up, and the young man she was tailing seemed to crisscross it like anything. He went down a small, unlit path at one point, and Susan, rather than charge in, waited at the end. The man stopped a few times, looking back, but Susan was out of sight.

She followed him carefully until he came to the run-down house. The front door was boarded up, as were two windows upstairs. He disappeared down the side and into the back garden. There, Susan saw a shed, which he entered. There was only one window at the side that Susan could make out, and no light was switched on in the shed.

Quickly, Susan texted her position to the team before taking up a position in the nearby shrubbery. She could feel the damp running in through her knees. The cold had her body. She pulled the three-quarter length leather jacket tighter around her.

What was he doing in there? From her position in the shrubbery, Susan could see the road beside the house, and two girls were walking along it. Susan could make out what looked like crop tops, or the excuse for tops, underneath their jackets. The skirts were so high; she wondered their legs weren't blue with cold.

The girls walked, their feet clipping along in high heels, the height of which made them unusable if you wanted to run and caused you to walk funny. Susan never saw the point in those sorts of heels. She liked small heels, or no heel at all. But she was an action kind of girl. At least that's what she told herself.

Two young women, one blonde, one brunette, approached the shed from the road but stopped for a smoke. The cigarettes once lit were like little orange beacons in the night. However, they had got closer and by a street light, Susan was able to see them more clearly. They were young. Really young. Twelve? Thirteen? Maybe? Or were they just dressed to look a lot younger? No, she thought. They're not developed. We develop as we grow. The womanly curve isn't there yet. They can only be thirteen, fourteen tops.

As she hid in the shrubbery, Susan could hear the girls beginning to talk.

'Who do you think it's going to be this time? That last one had a massive belly on him. Do you remember? Remember?'

'Remember it jiggling. I remember him watching you.'

'How about the other one? Do you remember his sitting beside you? All he wanted to do was sit and talk to you. He was really weird.'

The girls dragged hard on their cigarettes, laughing loudly while talking about a subject Susan found repulsive. They were also clearly nervous. Very nervous. Probably rightly so. They were too young to be in this position. A position no woman should be in. But they were dressed for the part. Her mother would have said they looked like a couple of tarts. There was a fine line, Susan thought, between looking sexy, between looking stylish, and looking like you weren't worth anything.

She wondered where the rest of the team were. She'd called them after all, wondering how this would develop. The girls, she reckoned, were coming here to meet the young man, but he was inside the shed. They had been on a path towards it, yet they'd stopped to smoke their cigarettes. But they were nearly done.

When they finished, the girls lit another one.

'Did you get that album?' One said to the other.

'Got more than that. Got a lot of stuff with what we earned last time.'

Getting paid. Paid to do this. That's why they're keeping quiet. What can you buy that's worth doing this? she thought. But then people did that, didn't they? People wanted things. Sometimes they didn't know why they wanted it. They were told they needed it. Knew that they wanted it.

She looked at the phones the girls had. They were top of the range. Susan wondered what she should do. Part of her wanted to step out, take the girls to one side, and ask about what they were doing. But she wouldn't have a link to the young man. They were standing on the street outside the shed. They were only ten yards away. But they hadn't made a beeline for it. And if they turned around and said they were just out and about, Susan would have nothing, and the link would be blown. She hunkered down again, waiting for a moment.

When the second cigarette was done, thrown to the ground and stamped on, the girls turned, looked at each other, and pulled their jackets back. There was some adjustment of clothing which clearly wasn't showing enough, before the jackets were pulled over again and they walked towards the shed. As they did so, they almost giggled.

It was a nervous giggle, a worried giggle, in some ways like they were doing something that had to be done to get something, but they weren't that sure about doing it. Susan watched the shed. There was no light, but the door was opening. As it did so, Susan saw the young man exit. His right hand was the last to leave, and it was only when it came out of the shed that Susan saw there was a blade in it.

By the streetlight, she saw the gleam of the orange glow across the blade. It was a machete, and it was ready to be swung. Susan would never reach in time, but she looked down, saw a small-size rock, and grabbed it. With everything she had, she threw it hard as the man's arm was raised with the machete to come down at the girls.

The throw was good, clocking him right on the side of the head. He was stunned for a moment, stumbled backwards, and the girls screamed.

Susan raced forward, noting, though, that the machete hadn't left his hand. She shouted at the girls to go, but she needn't have bothered, because they were off, clipping their way down the road in their ridiculous heels.

Susan reached up with two hands as his arm came down. She grabbed the wrist of the hand holding the machete, keeping it from her, trying to force it backwards. She felt him drive his other arm into her side. Susan was tight in, and so the punch wasn't delivered correctly. Then he was pulling her hair. She pulled the hand holding the machete towards her, and as it got close, she freed her hair and bit him hard on the wrist.

He howled, the machete dropping behind him, clanging, but he was strong, and now with his other hand he picked her up and threw her hard across the garden. She stumbled back and then fell, tumbling to the ground.

'You bitch! I've got to go after them now, you bloody bitch!'

Susan was groggy and watched as the man turned to grab hold of the machete, but then there was a foot stamping on the man's hand. He was dropped to the ground quickly, and a tall person started putting handcuffs on him.

As Susan groggily became aware, she could see that the red ponytail of Hope was bouncing freely as she struggled to put the cuffs on the young man.

'Two girls,' said Susan. 'Two girls, young, quite young, twelve, fourteen, something like that, running away in high heels. Need to get them, need to get them, they're involved in this.'

'Perry, Ross, get after them,' shouted Hope.

Susan was dazed, her head swimming, as she watched the form of Perry race past her. She put an arm down to the ground, not sure if she was going to remain conscious or not. He'd thrown her with such force.

* * *

They'd got there just in time. Perry had driven like a bat out of hell, because this was Susan, and this was not a nice estate. Now, he'd hurtled from beside her, chasing a couple of young women in high heels. Surely even Ross and he should be able to catch them. Perry ran harder than Ross, not because he was lighter, but because Ross never seemed to take off at pace. He wasn't an action man. Perry, although he didn't always seem to have the physical fitness, always seemed to be in the thick of the action. Looking down the road, he could see the two girls.

'Stop, police!' he shouted. 'We need to talk to you, we need to—'

And they cut down an alleyway. *Was it between two houses?* Perry raced along. As he got to the end, he looked left and saw both girls down there, still clipping along in their heels.

'This way, Ross.'

Perry ran along and then saw the girls split at the end of the row. He turned back to see Ross at the end of the passageway they'd entered.

'Go round,' he said, showing with his arm in a curling motion. 'Go round the side. One went that way; one this way.'

Ross should run into the other one, if he did it right, but Perry would have to get after his one.

As he reached the end of the passageway, he realised that she'd dropped the heels. She was now barefoot. The pavements were such that you could run on them without too much damage to your feet. There were no lots of stones around, things to make you yell. But Perry was now struggling for breath. He kept going, and in the distant lamplight he saw her. She was now cutting across a field. Perry cut her off. He went careering into the driveway of the house, through the back, where a man at the back door shouted at him.

'It's the police!' he said, charging along. He got to the hedge and dived through it, tumbling into some muck at the far side.

But he was in the field now, at the back of the estate. He could see her. She was running hard across, looking to get out down to the canal side beyond him.

Perry tore across the field running as hard as he could. And then, just within reach of her, he threw himself. The hands went out, wrapping around the young girl's shins as her feet came together. She tripped, face going smack into the ground. As Perry clung on to her legs, his shoulder hit hard, but he had her.

'Bastard,' she said, and she reached down, pulling his hair. She wasn't strong, though. Perry reached up with a hand, grabbing her wrist. He took it behind her and then pushed her over to get her other wrist. Soon he had the handcuffs on her. He sat up on his knees, puffing heavily.

'Right, love,' he said. 'We're going to walk back. You're not going to struggle. You're not in trouble, but we need to talk to you.'

She looked at him and spat in his face. Perry wiped, and then pushed her along, maybe a touch stronger than he should have done, as she stumbled across the field. He retraced his steps back towards the shed. Hope had brought the car up, and in the rear sat the young man they'd started tailing earlier on in the day. Susan was sitting in the front seat. As Perry approached, he gave her the thumbs up, and she nodded. *Well, thank goodness for that; at least she was okay.*

Hope smiled at him, and then pointed, and he saw Ross standing with a young girl, Ross looked deeply uncomfortable, and no wonder, as there was now a little bit of a crowd forming. Ross went for the other car and brought it up, and he and Perry put the two girls in the rear before climbing into the front seats of the car.

'We're going to take you to the station. You're not under arrest; however, you will be interviewed. We will ask you questions about the man in the shed and about what you're doing out tonight. You will, of course have representation. We can call family and friends, whatever you need.'

On the drive back, Perry wondered how they looked. Two men, the age of him and Ross with these two girls in the back, dressed like, well, what were they dressed like? Perry thought they didn't look even like hookers. They were too young. It was just wrong. It was weird. He pitied them and wondered what made them do it.

When they arrived at the station, Perry and Ross took them inside, ready for their interviews. They were allowed to clean up, and female police officers were placed with them until their parents would arrive. Meanwhile, Perry went to see Susan.

'You okay?' he asked.

'Yes. Nearly too late, though. I didn't think he'd have a machete on him. I thought he was going to sell them on.'

'He said they needed to end the problem. They're the problem. Come on,' said Perry.

'What?'

'We need to pick up Rupert. Hope's going to remain here with the girls. Macleod will come in with her. Ross, no doubt, will try to get every detail under the sun about them. You and I? Well, we need to pick Rupert up, ask him some questions. A lot of answering to do. See, Angus Morton was into young women. Macleod found that out. And here are a couple of young women for him.'

'Well, you're driving,' said Susan. 'I'm shattered. I need my bed.'

'You never sleep on this job,' said Perry.

Susan punched him in the arm. 'You slept this afternoon.'
'That's timing,' said Perry. 'You need to learn timing.'

Chapter 17

Macleod sat in the interview room with Hope beside him and Rupert Worrilow across from them. The man looked nervous, very nervous. Unlike Stephen Collins, the other younger man who was brought in, who was as cool as a cucumber, saying nothing, and insisting on a lawyer.

The two girls, however, were a little more chatty. The team discovered they were underage and so had been left with trained staff waiting for their parents to be contacted. Their age meant they technically had done nothing wrong rather, they were used.

'Tell me, Rupert, why are you panicking? What did you say to Stephen Collins? He left after speaking to you in the bushes, I might add,' said Macleod, 'hidden away from the public. He left you before making several phone calls and then waiting in a shed for the arrival of two young girls.'

'I don't know the names.'

'But why were you contacting Stephen, and why was he attempting to finish off the girls?'

'It's because, well, it's because of Angus.'

'Angus Morton?' asked Macleod.

'Angus knew them well. Stephen knew them, of course.'

'What has Angus got to do with it?' asked Hope.

'Angus, well, Angus liked that sort of thing. Contrary to popular belief, it wasn't young men that Angus liked. It was young girls. Very young girls.'

'And you what? Supply them?' asked Hope.

'We were up here and…, he asked about it. He asked me on the quiet. He knows a few things about me. Could get me moved on from the job.'

'What sort of things?' asked Hope.

'Things I've said about certain people in the business. Nothing illegal. I haven't done anything illegal.'

'Apart from procuring underage girls for sex,' said Macleod.

'I didn't. I put him in contact with Stephen.'

'But you knew what Stephen was going to be doing for him,' said Macleod.

'Yes, look, they seemed willing. Stephen always said they were always willing.'

'That's not really the point, is it?' said Macleod. 'Stephen doesn't give two hoots about those girls. He was ready to kill them.'

'I didn't tell him to kill them! I told him to make them go away. He was meant to pay them off. It was Stephen's decision to kill them. I had nothing to do with that.'

'So, Angus was shot, and you decided you needed to make this go away,' said Macleod.

'Well, you guys were all over it, weren't you? And if that sort of scandal got exposed, well, knowing what he was, everybody would go down. Everybody would be in hook, line, and sinker. I did it for him only once, only up here.'

'And how do you know Stephen Collins?' asked Macleod.

'I've done some drugs in the past. A former dealer put me in touch with him, said he dealt in that sort of thing.'

'According to some of my colleagues,' said Macleod, holding a report in front of him, 'Stephen has links to people smuggling and operates out of a lot of rather dubious areas.'

'I didn't know all that about him. I barely know the man at all. Angus told me I was to keep everything incredibly quiet. Apparently, Stephen could do that.'

'Well, he does that. Hasn't been caught, well, until now,' said Macleod, 'so I guess we can thank you for that.'

'Will I get pulled in for this?' asked Rupert.

'You're an accessory, the one who ultimately went about procuring these girls for Angus. You may not have done the act, but you were aware of it and did nothing to stop it. And you also engaged someone to make it happen,' said Hope. 'You won't walk away from it. If you're open and honest about everything, they might go more leniently on you.'

'How long have you known that Angus had these tastes?' asked Macleod.

'A while now,' said Rupert. 'Well, suspected as much. It's only when I came to work with him that I realised that this was the way he was, the truth of it. He was nasty. He knew things about me. Knew things about what I'd done on the stage. Things I'd said about people. Said he would use them. And of course, if he said it, everybody would believe it to be true. So…, so I went, and I got a hold of a couple of young women for him.'

'Girls,' said Macleod. 'I'm not sure they qualify as women yet.'

Rupert bent over. 'Oh God,' he said. 'What have I done?'

'Can you think of anyone who would want Angus dead then?

Is there any way that the parents of these girls found out?' asked Hope.

'Not that I'm aware of. Stephen didn't say so. Stephen said it was all done on the quiet. That was it. We were just leaving it at that. Angus and he made the arrangements. Stephen was making good money out of him. So, I doubt Stephen would have killed him. No real point.'

That was true, Macleod conceded to himself. Stephen Collins would want this arrangement to keep going. And if the worst of it threatened to come out, he could bribe Angus and make more money off him.

'I'm not one to kill people. I'm not one to finish them. Even these two girls. Although I never met them, I didn't want them dead. I said to Stephen, just make it go away. He decided they had to be killed.'

'Did he tell you he was going to kill them?'

'No,' said Rupert, 'but, well, this is the company I'm dealing with now, isn't it?'

Macleod left the room and looked in again on Stephen. After ten minutes, he left that interview with Hope, because Collins was refusing to say anything. They spent the next hour, once the parents of the young girls had been found, interviewing the girls. They seemed to think everything was great fun, and they enjoyed the money. Their parents were horrified, but the girls seemed to be relaxed.

'The old man couldn't do much, anyway.'

'Did he hurt you in any way?' asked Macleod.

'No, a lot of it he just wanted to watch. It's a bit of fun; we earned a lot of money.'

'But he had sex with you?' asked Macleod.

'Yes,' said one girl, quite brightly. 'It's an easy way to afford things.'

When Macleod left those interviews, he was feeling sorry for the parents. They were raging, yet the girls had seemed quite unrepentant. They'd had a close escape, for Stephen Collins was known for people smuggling. Maybe the girls would have been moved on elsewhere. They could have been dead as well, if not for Susan's attentions.

As Macleod climbed the stairs back up to his office, he was flagged by Ross from the team office.

'Come in, please, sir. Got something for you.' Macleod walked over to Ross's desk and was soon joined by Hope.

'We're looking into the links for the guns and mechanisms. The two stagehands have done prop work before, but I have got nothing that links them directly to guns. Not firing them, not using them anywhere else. That's not to say they haven't done any reenactments or they haven't set up props. So yes, they could have an interest in mechanisms. However,' said Ross, 'Sandra Brown is a bit of an expert. She trained with firearms in a previous role. And also, our director, Frances Jollye, is also a club shooter. She uses nothing high-calibre, as per current government club rules. But she knows how to shoot.'

'And you've got nothing on anyone else?'

'No,' said Ross. 'I also looked into stands for guns. They're not that common. I've been talking to our ballistics expert, who was working with Jona, and we're not sure that we can get a stand for the weapon that was used. We've narrowed it down to the sort of weapon, but he's thinking more of a custom build, not a standard issue, certainly at the height that the gun was fired from.'

'So you're telling me that somebody made this?' asked

Macleod.

'That's what it looks like. It's to do with those screw-downs into the holes in the stage. According to the ballistics expert, nothing comes like that. That's special, and the height's wrong. You would want to fire it from higher up. It's sort of an in-between height if you had a stand, and you want to be behind the sight. Looking at where you're aiming, you would be down flat on your belly looking up, or you'd be looking from a standing position behind it. He doesn't know of a stand for an automatic firing rig either. You would still aim though. It would be a support to you.'

'Thank you, Ross,' said Macleod. He wandered over to Hope's office, and she followed him in. After making a coffee, the two sat and thought together.

'I guess Morton could have wound up many people if he was up to that sort of game,' said Hope.

'I don't think he's done that sort of game too often. He's very careful about what he says. When he talked to Jameson in Glasgow, he didn't push the issue. He got out of the way. He's also got Rupert to do his legwork on this. It's not common knowledge that's the way he was, where his tastes lay.'

'No,' said Hope, 'but it doesn't mean that someone didn't know. That someone could have found out. That it could have come from his past.'

'It would be a good reason to kill him,' said Macleod, 'irrespective of what's happening with the stage or the production or anything else. It would be a good reason.'

'Still, we need to ask the question, though, how does it get set up? It must have come from inside. It can't have been Rupert that did it, because he had no real reason. As far as he was aware, Angus Morton was happy with him. He'd done his bit for him, and that was that. It was only when Angus was shot that he went off the rails and pulled in Stephen.'

'That's true,' said Macleod. 'Rupert's not looking that good as a murderer. If you look at the two who could have shot him, or had the skills and the weapons, why Frances? Makes no sense. She's doing really well. Sandra, too, is a jobbing actor. What! She finally got so sick of him she just shot him? She's too old to have been a younger girl for him at some point. I don't think that's working either.'

'Well, maybe we need to talk to them,' said Hope. 'Try to establish if they had any children or nieces that maybe were preyed upon by Angus.'

'You have to be careful, though,' said Macleod. 'Just because that was his appetite doesn't mean that's why he was killed. He was also a gambler, remember?'

'He's not really a role model you want your kids to look up to, is he?'

'No,' said Macleod. 'But we keep all of this quiet as well. I can't have this leaking out to the press. It could cause somebody to run, to get away. I don't want people to know we're coming after them.'

'We don't have anybody to go after yet. Let's go talk to Sandra, first of all,' said Hope. 'That would make sense.'

'Where is she at the moment?' asked Macleod.

'Last I heard, she was in her hotel room. That's where most of them have stayed before looking to move on. By the sound of it, they may just be doing that.'

'Well, let's go,' said Macleod. He took a walk upstairs, grabbed his jacket, came back down the stairs, and met Hope, coming out of her office. Together, they descended and went out the rear door of the police station. Just as they were getting in the car, though, Susan Cunningham pulled up in her own car.

'Are you two off somewhere?' she asked.

'Just going to talk to Sandra at the hotel,' said Hope.

'Well, I think you should go there. But you'll not be able to talk to Sandra.'

'But we need to. Ross has just confirmed that she's able to handle a gun. We need to know whether she's got that ability. She needs to tell us what she's done with a gun before.'

'Well, that's going to be difficult,' said Susan. 'She's dead in her hotel room. Apparently, they found a suicide note.'

'What? Sandra?' blurted Macleod.

'All I know at the moment is she's dead and there was a suicide note. I came racing back here to get you.'

'Get the rest of the team,' said Macleod. 'Get everyone down to the hotel. We want to secure the rest of them.'

'I warn you,' said Susan, 'the press are already gathering outside that hotel. They've been there anyway, wanting to interview them all.'

'Blast it,' said Macleod.

'You couldn't have seen it coming,' said Hope. 'I mean, who'd have known she'd have such a motive?'

'She doesn't have a motive,' said Macleod. 'She doesn't have any motive at all. She's the next victim. We just need to work out why.'

Chapter 18

Macleod sat impassively in the car as Hope slowly drove him through the press cordon around the hotel. As he exited the car, he could hear the shouts. 'Why is this one dead? Detective Chief Inspector. Oi, Macleod, why haven't you got the killer yet? How many more will die? What's going on with this one?'

Macleod hated the press. They were always there asking questions before you'd even seen what had happened. And there was always a thing that the second body was your fault. Not the first one, but because you were on the case, the second one happened because you weren't doing the right thing. Of course, that was nonsense. Together with Hope, he entered the hotel, took the lift to the third floor and walked along to where there were two policemen standing outside a room.

'Miss Nakamura's inside,' said one constable. 'She's asked for no one to go in.'

'Of course,' said Macleod. He leaned around the constable and, shouted. 'Jona! Seoras! We need to speak.'

Thirty seconds later, a fully hooded and suited, Jona Naka-mura came out into the hallway. She pulled down her coverall hood and looked up at Macleod. 'I am here. Speak.'

'What have you got for me?'

'You come all the way up to my room,' said Jona, 'and you haven't even got a coverall on yet.' She tutted, entered the room again, came out and threw two coveralls at them. 'If you get dressed up, you can come in,' she said.

About two minutes later, Macleod and Hope entered the room. It was a standard hotel room, with a double bed on one side, a desk with a lamp, a minibar—which when Macleod examined it, seemed to be half empty—and a note sitting on the table.

'This the suicide note,' said Macleod.

'Yes,' said Jona. *'Terrible tragedy. Sad to see my friend go. Don't feel I can live with it anymore.* I'm not a handwriting expert,' said Jona. 'I'm also not a psychiatrist, but personally, I think that's a load of waffle. And I don't think it's written by her.'

Macleod looked over at a chair and saw Sandra's body draped over it.

'How did she die?' asked Macleod.

'Well, looks like she's been poisoned.'

'Where's the poison come from?'

'There's residue from a cup on the floor I've sent off for testing. I expect to get a positive result from it.'

'So there's residue in a cup. She must have drunk it; therefore, she's made it herself, in which case suicide seems reasonable, or she's drunk it with somebody else, or has been unaware of it. Are there any other cups in the room?' asked Macleod.

'No,' said Jona. He looked down at the belongings of Sandra. The wardrobe had been opened. Clothes had been gone through. Photographs taken.

'It makes little sense,' said Macleod.

'No,' said Hope. 'Why would you commit suicide?'

'She's got nothing to commit it for. She's been murdered,' said Macleod. 'Sandra was quite open about Angus, though, believed his behaviour and his conduct were very suspect. She tried to warn me about it. So why be like this? What's the point?'

'We could look at who came in,' said Hope.

'Of course,' said Macleod. 'Need to talk to the others, obviously. It's not Rupert, is it? We need to have a look, though. Did Helen come in here? Alistair? Frances? Dieter? Julie? Who of all of them came in here?'

'When were they in too, because something was slipped into her cup?' said Hope.

'Well, that's what Jona's going with, so let's talk to our director,' said Macleod. 'There's nothing more to achieve here until Jona comes up with something.'

They stepped out of the room, took off their coveralls, and made their way along the corridor to a room at the end. This was being guarded by a police constable as well. He rapped on the door, which then opened, and he advised Frances Jollye that the detective inspector was here to talk to her.

'Come in, Inspector.' Macleod entered and watched Frances take up a seat in the far corner of the room.

'I take it you've heard,' said Macleod.

'Yes,' said Frances. 'Both my lead actors are dead. What's the point? Never going to get it up and going again. I can't just start filling in for a couple of actors. One, maybe, get it up and going. But two, especially two of the main ones, it will not work.'

'Did you know about Angus Morton's sexual leanings?'

'There was all that story about him being gay, but it didn't really wash with me. I'm not sure what his real passions would be.'

'Well,' said Macleod, 'he was actually being fed young women. One of your troupe put him in contact with a man who deals in that line of work.'

'Well, it wasn't Sandra that did it,' said Frances. 'Sandra ran a campaign to protect younger women in the industry. She was very against it. There's been such a history of it in the past. It's still there, if we're honest. I guess sometimes I get it a bit easier because if I'm asking for certain type of scenes that require little or no clothing, they don't think, why am I doing it? They think I'm doing it for the plot, which is why I am doing it, of course. But a male director may not get that opportunity to explain why he's doing it.'

'Sandra ran a campaign?' said Macleod.

'I don't think it was smoke and mirrors. I think she genuinely meant it.'

'Did she ever say anything about Angus?' asked Hope.

'She didn't like him from that point of view. But she called him a consummate professional. She always said that about him, but really did not like the way he treated other actors. Sandra hated how he hung around some of the younger members of the crew. Helen, for instance. He was quite, well, maybe I would say leery but maybe it was just his age. Different times, different ages, you know. I'm not sure.'

'On a different note,' said Hope. 'I believe you can handle firearms.'

'I've been in a gun club. Sandra could fire weapons, too. She told me she'd trained up when she did a film a while ago. What of it?'

'Well, Angus Morton was shot, wasn't he?'

'Yes, but I would have had to have shot him from the rear of the theatre. Up by the desk. I couldn't have gone into the wings and shot from there and run back out again. Besides, I was seen. A lot of the public saw me.'

'We believe that it may have been an automated weapon, not one that was fired at the time by a human. It may have required setting up though, and the shooter would have to understand how the mechanics work.'

'I can't do that,' blurted Frances. 'I don't do mechanics. When we fire a gun at the gun club, and it's usually a rifle, most of the time it's set up for me. I don't have to work a lot with it. I do it only as a little pastime, and I don't get to do it that often because I'm usually touring with a production.'

'So you're saying to me,' clarified Macleod, 'that you wouldn't be able to put a gun on a stand and make it fire?'

'Do I look like one of those people?' said Frances. 'If I need something to work, if I need a prop or something to happen, I have got a stage crew. They come up with many wonderful ways to make things work. You need to understand that, it's not me.'

'And in the play, who decided where Angus would stand?'

'Angus did. He had a free rein about where to stand at what times, how he said things. Yes, I gave him a little cajoling here, there and wherever. But I basically needed to let him get on with it.'

'But once he'd gone to the same place, he would always go to the same place?'

'That's the way it works,' said Frances. 'You drill, you rehearse. People don't realise how much of the rehearsal is being in the right place at the right time for different things. That's why we mark the floor sometimes. Also to bring the props on to the proper place.'

'And so,' said Macleod, 'he would have been there, in that same spot, at the same time of the play. Each and every night.'

'Well, that's what you try to do. You try not to make anything different, but things sometimes go awry. Look, Inspector, I know nothing about either death. Besides, your guys said there was a suicide note. Somebody mentioned a suicide note.'

'There may have been a suicide note,' said Macleod, 'but that means nothing until we've verified that it is actually that. And it was written by the victim, not whoever killed her.'

'When was the last time you saw Sandra?' asked Hope.

'I can't be sure exactly, but I have seen her over the last day or two. There was still a need to discuss things. She's the most senior actress I've got at the moment, so I needed to talk things through with her, especially about getting somebody else in. Any ideas, names. It's not that easy.'

'Did you get a list of names?' asked Macleod.

'Well, yes, but I haven't gone around them all yet. You've got to know they're available. They've got to be willing. There's so much to do to coordinate somebody else coming in. You've got to know that they can get up to the mark within a couple of weeks and not have disputes with anyone else. This death is just completely untimely for me,' said Frances. 'And now another one's ruined me. I mean that.'

Macleod looked around the room. There were a couple of cups sitting beside a kettle, but the cups differed from those within Sandra's room. He wondered why.

'Have you had anybody in here?' asked Macleod.

'Well, I've met people.'

'Do you offer them a cuppa?'

'No. Not here. If I want to do that, we'll go downstairs, we'll book a room and we'll sit down with tea and whatever and discuss. I just pop in. People don't come to me. They know I don't like to be disturbed. So, I go to them.'

'Did you go to Sandra recently?'

'Well, I just told you I did, trying to sort out what to do with the tour.'

'Sandra could use a weapon,' said Hope. 'You think Sandra could have killed him? And now she's made an exit.'

'No. No, no,' said Frances. 'As I said, she was staunch. She ran the campaign to protect young women. The last thing she's going to do is just kill the man and not announce it if that's the case. Why would she?'

Indeed, thought Macleod. *Why would you?* There was nothing in the suicide note to say that was what she'd done. There were no regrets from that point of view.

'Look,' said Frances. 'Everything's gone to pot now. We're going to struggle to bring this production back online again. Why don't you just let us go?'

'Not yet,' said Macleod. 'Not yet.'

'Guess we're waiting on Jona to come up with something,' said Hope as they left the room.

'Did you notice something?' said Macleod.

'What?'

'The cups in there, they're different from those in Sandra's.'

'And?'

'Different cups. Just something I noticed. There's only one cup in Sandra's room. So, I'm wondering if, well, is that one of her cups? Or is it somebody else's cup? Or did somebody have to take her cups away to then bring them back?'

'It wouldn't be that difficult to access a cup, would it?' said Hope. 'Cleaning ladies are here and there, leaving their trolleys in the middle of the corridor. You could soon swipe a cup off them.'

'You're right, but what bothers me more is the fact that Sandra's now dead. For some reason, Sandra clocked what was going on. At least, that's my theory. I don't see why anybody else wants her dead. If you want the show to go on, you don't want to kill Sandra. She's needed. If you need your pay packet at the end of the day, she's needed. She is needed for this production. So, if someone's killed her, it's because she knew something.'

Macleod left the hotel to return to the office. As he got to the line of press, he was half accosted, a microphone stuck into his face.

'Detective Chief Inspector, some people have said you're not on top of this case. Some people have said that this murder is clearly the—'

Macleod put his hand up in front of the man's microphone and closed his fist around it.

'Quiet,' said Macleod. 'Got work to do.'

He then walked on, hearing the cries of, 'You're not saying anything to me because you have nothing to say.'

Macleod fumed. He couldn't stand much of the press. You got the odd press person who was okay, making an honest living. Difficult in that world. But he also knew there were plenty there. The longer a case went on, and especially if it was full of juicy murders, in some ways the press would like it. From a business sense, if you took all the emotion out, it was perfect. After all, that's what the news was. It was sensationalism. It was a scandal. Things that you didn't get in your normal everyday life. That was the whole point of it.

He gave a sigh as he got into the car, and Hope jumped in on the other side. She started up the engine and then turned to look at him.

'You look terrible,' she said.

'Well, thanks very much,' said Macleod. 'You don't know how much that boosts me.'

'I mean it. You're not good at doing these all-nighters.'

'You're not wrong there,' said Macleod. 'I'm not going to miss the press either.'

'You just need to handle them better. You're always antagonistic,' said Hope.

'And you're what, lovey-dovey with them?'

'No, but I let them play their games. Play them with them. And then play them back,' said Hope.

'Can't be bothered with the dance,' said Macleod. 'Whirling here and there, just trying to keep them on their toes, and the information they cry out for, often, so ordinary people can keep that.'

'Do you ever think Jane would have been good with the press?' asked Hope.

'She couldn't have been any worse than I,' said Macleod. 'She has a face for people. Always jolly, always looking like she's on top of things.'

'Well, make sure she comes with you to your farewell day. Can't have your moping face there the whole time.'

'Drive,' said Macleod. He hadn't even laughed at it, just grumbled and told her to get on with it. Maybe it was because things were getting older, stale. Most of all, him.

Chapter 19

We need to move on this,' said Macleod, his eyes scanning the rest of the team. 'A second person's died because they knew something.'

'There's no link?' asked Perry. 'Are we sure there's no link from one to the other? You think it's a cover-up for the murder?'

'Well, that's my feeling,' said Macleod. 'Ross hasn't come up with anything, have you?'

'They're actors. They've worked together occasionally, but there's nothing else linking them. Nothing else says they were good friends.'

'I got the feeling Sandra was a consummate professional working alongside Angus Morton,' said Macleod. 'Angus Morton, especially with these rumours about young women, would cause a problem for Sandra. She ran a campaign, according to Frances, a campaign for better protection for girls coming into the theatre. It wouldn't sit well being pals with Angus, being too close to him, if there're rumours about him in the background.'

'But those rumours must have been well held,' said Perry. 'He's a national treasure. You don't stay a national treasure if there're things like that in the air.'

'So, are we on the right track with this? Are we on the right track in saying that Angus's involvement with underage girls is the motive for murder? Is it simple revenge?'

'One thing that makes sense,' said Hope, 'is that Sandra could have exposed him if she already knew what he was. She would have looked to expose him. After all, she was running this campaign, and even if she didn't particularly believe in it, the very least it would have given her was kudos amongst the acting community. It would have lifted her up. In saying that, there's no reason to suggest that she didn't believe in it, in which case she would have outed him unless she could not prove it. There's no point in killing somebody off if they're not able to prove something against you. That just doesn't make sense.'

'So, what did she know?' asked Macleod. 'What's put her in the firing line?'

'Maybe, she saw something when the gun's fired, said Hope. 'The stand? Somebody building it beforehand? Maybe it's about the way she knew something or somebody thought she knew something. They don't always have to know. People just have to suspect.'

'What about CCTV footage?' said Susan. 'Do we have some?'

'There'll be something to go over.'

'Then you do it,' said Macleod. 'You go through that, Hope.'

'But getting back to my point,' said Hope. 'If she knew something, if she knew how this was done, well that would be a reason to kill. Maybe she discovered something. I was thinking about this. We're talking about a stand for a weapon. If it's automatically done and the gun fires, you've still got to get rid of it from backstage. Now, nobody from our stage crew or the actors leaves, but what if you hide it? What if you hide it in plain sight? Have we gone through that stage? Have we checked the trapdoors? Have we checked hidey-holes? Maybe it's in plain sight.'

'Then we search again,' said Macleod, 'We search again. Hope, you get onto the CCTV. Take Ross with you. Perry, Susan, you're with me. We're going to go down and search that theatre again.'

Five minutes later, Macleod was in his own car, driving round to the theatre. It wasn't far to travel, but everywhere he went, he could see press. The nation was captivated by this mystery, especially now with Sandra dead too. He'd have to do a press briefing soon.

Macleod used to enjoy sending Hope off to give a conference, but he didn't want her face at the front of this one. He needed to be there. If they couldn't get to the bottom of it, if it took time, or there was something nasty that came from it, he wanted it all to reflect on him, not Hope. She needed to have a good start, especially with the new DCI coming in. This was his parting gift to her, because this one could get nasty.

Macleod waited for Perry and Susan before entering the theatre. There was still a police presence around it, and the place had been sealed off since that night. Inside the main auditorium, he took a moment to think again about what had happened.

Sandra would have been on the stage. But what could she see? How would it feel to be on stage? After all, the lights would blaze but your eyes would be accustomed to that. You'd then look back to the wings, and it'd be dark. Getting your bearings, getting to see things back there might be difficult. Could it be that Sanda saw something there?

Macleod walked into the backstage area. Here and there, there were props still lying around. But it was, in truth, fairly clean. Walking over to where the three holes were, and where the gunshot had come from, he looked up. Lighting rigs, curtains and backdrops to fall down. There was a gantry up there, and he made his way up, holding the handrails as he walked across. He wasn't great with heights, and when somebody had been murdered, it always set him on edge, even though it was his job to look into it.

'I can't see anything down here,' said Perry. 'There's the rig, there are the chairs, there're props, bits of scenery to come in.'

'Search through them. Anything that's a stand, anything that could be used like a stand.'

'Gone underneath as well,' said Susan, springing up on the stage. 'I can't see anything underneath. Trying to find a stand, trying to find something that would hold a gun. There's no gun either. It's no good. I mean, they could have removed it anyway by then, couldn't they?'

'No,' said Macleod, 'it's here. It hasn't gone out of the building. They had to walk out with it. Our actors and our backstage crew didn't walk out with anything. And Jona has had this place sealed since. The whole place has been protected.'

'Well, we got nothing,' said Susan.

'Right, I'm going to find our director. Find out what goes on back here. I need to understand how they could hide it.'

'What do you want us to do?' asked Perry.

'Keep going,' said Macleod. He came down from the upstairs rig and left, giving a nod to the police constable in the front doorway. They would keep the place sealed. Outside, there were a few press folk, but most had moved to the hotel.

'Has this one got you beat, Inspector?' said a voice.

'Investigations are continuing,' said Macleod.

'Second death, though. Are there going to be more?'

'I don't actually carry them out,' said Macleod. 'I just find out who does them, and bring them to justice.'

'You're sounding a little rattled,' said the journalist.

'As I said, investigations are continuing.'

Macleod climbed into his car, and he almost swore at the man. It wasn't like him. Macleod was calm, especially in something like this. He understood sometimes he got worked up when there were kids involved or a particularly gruesome murder. This one just seemed to rattle for no reason. No, there was a reason. He was just getting older.

He thought back to when he'd gone out to St Kilda, when Hope had successfully stayed alive with her family, when someone had sought to kill many rich people. Hope's little Ian had been put at risk, and Macleod had smacked the culprit right in the face, or at least one of them. That wasn't like him, but that's the way he was becoming now. Less restricted. It was an age thing, wasn't it? Now was the time to get out. Now was the time to go and not have so much pressure on you.

He was still a convivial man. He was still a man who enjoyed talking to people. As long as they were half sensible, of course. He enjoyed seeing little Ian. He would never be a granddad, so, being a godparent was as close as he was going to get. Hope was as close to a daughter as he'd come, but she was no daughter. Yet she was more than a colleague.

Macleod arrived at the hotel, where there were more press. This time he just gave a 'No comment' to any of the questions and slipped inside of the press cordon into the hotel. Hope was apparently locked away with the CCTV, so Macleod went up to Frances Jollye's room and knocked on the door. It took a while for her to answer. When she did, Macleod saw she was dressed in a pair of track bottoms and had pulled a t-shirt on.

'My apologies,' said Macleod. 'Were you asleep?'

'Didn't sleep well, when Sandra was killed. It's just been, well, hectic. I think I'm stuffed now.'

'My colleague is looking into Sandra's death at the moment,' said Macleod. 'I've just been back at the theatre and I'm trying to understand about backstage and what happens. You're the director, so I would expect that backstage you would run it, deciding where everything goes.'

'Well, only to a point. I've very much of an overview. The nitty-gritty is Dieter's realm.'

'Why is that?' asked Macleod.

'I've just so much else to do. I've got a cast to get acting. Someone's needed who's going to cover off all the other things. Make sure the props are there on time for one. We do have meetings, and we talk about what's needed and where it's meant to be. And when I'm on stage, when we're rehearsing, Dieter's there along with his stagehands.'

'So, if someone were to bring something in, if somebody wanted to hide something,' said Macleod.

'Hide something? Like what?' asked Frances.

'Like a stand.'

'A stand? For what?'

'For a gun. If someone were to bring a stand in for a gun, then wanted to hide it, who would know about it? Who could hide that successfully?'

'Well, I guess anybody could actually hide it. But I don't know where you would hide it. What, hide it amongst stuff?'

'What if you wanted to make it part of something? I'm

thinking,' said Macleod, 'that if this item was brought in—and imagine it's some sort of stand—then you couldn't get it back out for a few days. So, you want it to look like it's in plain sight. So, it's been there a couple of days, and then it goes back to not being there again. How would you do that? Who could do that? I'm also, I guess, asking who would know that something did or didn't belong?'

'The actors are going to struggle with that to understand what should and shouldn't be there,' said Frances. 'The backstage crew would know. I would know, in all honesty, I would think. Well, actually no I wouldn't. The best person to know would be Dieter. Dieter is in charge of all of that. Dieter's the one that goes through the fine detail, and yes, Peter and Julie do a lot, but Dieter is the one who's responsible.

'If Dieter goes around and sees something that isn't right, he'll pull it up. He should know the whole of that backstage inside out—but not just props, the lighting and the scenery, too. When we first arrive, he goes all over it. He's the one who helps us set up the stage. Now in truth it's not a complicated stage, this one, but there are backdrops and other things within it.'

'So, Dieter would know,' said Macleod.

'Yes,' said Frances. She gave a sigh and turned to walk over to the window of her bedroom.

'I take it all ideas of the production going on are probably halted now,' said Macleod.

'Would be hard to do, certainly to continue with the current dates and things,' said Frances. 'You could start again from the top, but well, you'd lose the momentum. Be hard to get them to back it; we'd need another Angus Morton on the front of it.'

'Well, I'm sorry,' said Macleod. 'Clearly you put a lot of work into it.'

'Not really that important, is it, not in the context?' said Frances. 'Two people are dead. I mean two people are dead, and you're acting as if it's one of us. That's kind of more worrying.'

'Do you know anything about the others? Is there anything you need to tell me?' asked Macleod.

'I'm a director, not a research assistant. I don't look into the depths of what's going on with people. Yes, I can bring their characters out on stage, but I'm there to get a production going. And in truth, I think it's all just hitting me. When can I head home?'

'I'd like you to stay for another couple of days. I'm trying to put some more of a police presence around you.'

'Well, I think I'd be safer at home.'

'Give me a few more days,' said Macleod, 'and then I will let you go, and you all disperse back.'

Macleod stepped out of the room and thought about what she'd said. Dieter would know, Dieter would understand. He had no reason to suspect that Dieter had done anything. There were no links to Dieter. Nobody had indicated, either within his own people or within the troop, that Dieter was involved. It wasn't mentioned that he could use a gun, but he would understand props.

He would take him, Macleod decided, take Dieter and Jona both—Jona to confirm what the man was saying. After all, he could be a hostile witness if he carried out the murder, but Jona would know the ins and outs of it. Jona could verify whether something could be made into a tripod to hold a gun. That's what he would do. He would take the person on his team who had the best ideas, best understanding, and match it with the best person on the troop.

Macleod had a theory. He had a theory about a remote-controlled weapon taking down Angus Morton. He needed to prove it, and strictly he was probably out of his field in doing it.

Chapter 20

'How's he doing, John?'

'He's fine. I got him his bottle. It's all working okay.'

'I should have checked in sooner. Is he pining? Does he need me?' asked Hope.

'What do you want me to say? You knew this was going to be tough for him. He'll have to get used to it. You're on a case. You can't come back. He's okay. He's getting fed, got enough milk. When you get back, we can sort out some more.'

Hope had wondered what it would be like, how difficult it would be. Little Ian had come into her life and had been so closely attached to her. Now she had to walk away from him to do another job. The job required so much focus that little indications, which before were pleasurable and a joy of motherhood, became an awkward distraction. She felt guilty about seeing them this way.

The thing about being a detective was that everybody thought you just switched into it. You didn't. It was so involved, especially in a case like this. You were all on the go; everyone was firing questions at you. Every time you stepped outside, the press was there. Every time you stepped into the station, the boss was there. Everyone was there asking what was going on. Your mind was constantly on it and then she would feel it, that moment for a feed.

All those subtle indications were in her body. She just knew when he wanted fed. And it had all been upturned because her whole routine had gone. It wasn't the case now of little Ian demanding to be fed. She had to prep the food in advance. Express for him and that wasn't the same. Had she come back too soon?

John had said no. John had said he could handle it. And he was handling it. And there was no other person she would have had there looking after her little one. But she felt guilty. Struggling between whether her place was here or there. In truth, she thought it was both. But how could that be?

'Are you with us?' asked Ross beside her.

'Sorry Alan, I've just been on the phone there.'

'It's okay, I know how you feel. It's okay.'

Does he really? thought Hope. *Alan's never had to feed his little one.* And then she felt guilty. *Of course he knows what it feels like, he's got his little boy, he has to come away from him.*

'Shall we get to work?' said Hope.

'Right,' said Ross, 'we've got the third floor, and on the third floor, you've got Sandra's room. The only other people up here are Angus and Frances. Frances wasn't meant to be up here, but the hotel had an issue, and Frances got put in a room up here. We have got CCTV going back and forward, so we can see over the last few days who's come and gone. Let's run it through,' said Ross.

Hope sat beside Ross, taking notes of the last days before Sandra died, running from after Angus had died, right through until Sandra's own death. Hope's notes said that she had been visited by Julie, Dieter, Frances, Alistair and Helen. But Hope noted that most of the visits were brief. Only Frances's seemed to last.

There was no CCTV inside the room, so Hope could only guess what had been said. She would go through and ask people, but in truth, most visits were so brief, it was almost like a call, except for Frances and one with Alistair. The one with Alistair wasn't surprising. They'd seemed close. Instead, Hope decided she would visit Frances. Knocking on the door, she heard a moan, and then the door was opened. Frances stood there. Her hair was a mess, and she was in a T-shirt and track bottoms.

'What do you want?' she said rather blearily.

'I need to talk to you. Sorry, were you asleep?'

'I only just got back to sleep. Your detective chief inspector was here not that long ago.'

'Well, I'm sorry,' said Hope. 'I've just been running through CCTV, and I need to ask you a few questions. Can I come in?'

'Why not?' said Frances. The woman left the door open for Hope and went to sit on her bed. Hope closed the door behind her and then walked over to the window of the hotel. She looked down.

'The vultures are still there,' said Frances. 'Used to clamour for all the press. Opening nights. You struggle to get them in; you struggle to get them excited. Have a murder and everybody wants to know about your play. Should have done it before.' Hope cast a glance over at her. 'Sorry. Not funny?'

'Certainly no laughing matter but I take your point,' said Hope. 'Do you think somebody would have done this for that reason? To generate profits, to generate—'

Frances looked at her. 'I didn't need to. None of us needed

to. It was going well.'

'You went to Sandra not long before she died but after the death of Angus. You were in there for quite a while.'

'Yes? It's true,' said Frances.

'What did you talk about?' asked Hope.

'Going on. The play, the production. She was my main actress. If she didn't do it, it was gone. The production was done. She had to continue. I needed her.'

'And what did she say?'

'It wasn't a case of just yes or no. We talked it through, but she was troubled, really troubled. She was talking about quitting. I've known Sandra for a while, and certainly, in the industry, when other directors talk about her, and producers, she is old school. The show must go on. She batters away, but she was talking about quitting. It's not like her, was not like her at all. She's one of the old warhorses.'

'Old? She was only forty-seven, wasn't she?' said Hope.

'When do you think you stop being of use as an actress?' asked Frances. 'It's a sexist industry. You can be an old, distinguished man like Angus and keep going. Sandra did well because she's just a wonderful actress. But if you're middle of the road, you know, you're okay, then you're into bit parts, you're into small pieces. Sandra was holding down parts that required a mature lady. But starring roles, who's starring alongside Angus in this one? Helen, and why?'

'What do you mean, why?'

Frances looked at Hope. 'Tell me. When you go out there amongst the press, who do they try to talk to? You or your boss?'

'I'm sorry?'

'Who do they want to talk to? You or your boss? Your boss

is quite, well, not exactly a sexy man, is he?'

'All right,' said Hope. 'Well, they want to talk to me, of course they do.'

'Yes, six feet tall. Red hair. Good body, if you don't mind me saying so.'

'Well, I'm not long after becoming a mother. Still trying to get it back in shape.'

'If that's you out of shape, then you have the jealousy of women everywhere,' said Frances. 'What I'm trying to say is Helen was our starring female in the eyes of the press. She can't act for toffee compared to Sandra. Sandra had the depth of soul to act. She could pull off amazing performances, and she had to because she was too old. Too old for the gutter boys out there. Instead, we have Helen. Producers said we wanted Helen in. Why? Well, she's been on telly. She's done a little bit of this, that and whatever. They know her. Sure. She's in the press. Do you know what she was in the press for?'

'Not really,' said Hope. 'She'd been on holiday recently, hadn't she? Did I see her in one of the papers?'

'Yes. Running commentary on her boobs,' said Frances. 'I actually had a production meeting where they were talking about how Helen would be dressed in the production. The character she plays is meant to be a fairly modest young woman. She's meant to be clever, which is why she ends up killing the guy. But no, I actually have notes. I'll get you my notebook that said, producer said, "Plenty of cleavage for Helen."'

'I didn't think that sort of thing happened anymore.'

'Well, he didn't put it like that, did he? He just said we need to show off her figure and said it was part of the character as he saw it. They don't turn around and say to you, "Needs big boobs." I bet they don't say to you, "You do the press because you've got a great backside."'

'Well, my boss tells me to do the press because he hates them,' laughed Hope. 'He just doesn't enjoy them at all. He puts me up because he knows I can handle them.'

'Then you're very lucky. He appreciates you for your abilities and not for how you look.'

Hope gave a smile. 'What was her decision? What was Sandra going to do?'

'I think she was going to quit,' said Frances. 'But it was unlike her. She'd gone through deaths of actors before. Admittedly, not murdered. But she'd carried productions through major issues before. Never quit. The show must go on. Consummate professional. I'll be there, love, she would say.'

'And she was upset about Angus's death? Do you think that could have been an issue?'

'She had no love for Angus. I knew that when I first saw them come together. Now on stage, you wouldn't have seen it. But during rehearsals and after, the others would crowd to him. The likes of Helen. She'd have gone close to Angus. Rupert, especially. But Sandra, no. Sandra was a distance apart. In truth, she was the better actor. She had more about her, more depth of character. Angus just hit the right vein. Had done all his life. Played the right parts and then became a national treasure. And then they don't really look at you. They don't really assess if you're running a product like that.'

'A product?' queried Hope.

'Oh yes, actors become a product. I mean, he's a national treasure at this point. What we can't do is bring him down. You get told that. You get told by producers that he has to fit into the image because that's what we're selling. We're selling the image. I just want to make a play, to tell a story. I want people to understand the good and the bad and make them think through what I put up on stage but no—producers are there to make money, and I get that.'

'What about Alistair? Alistair and she were quite close. They have a falling out at all or—'

'Alistair adored her, would follow her everywhere. Alistair would hang on to what she said because she was everything that Alistair hadn't managed to be. The man was all bit parts. Alistair did well to get this part in the play but he's a struggling actor, and someone like Sandra was a hero to him, and I don't blame him. She showed how to be in a role and not lose the plot, how to be yourself. A strong woman and fought for other women to be strong.'

'Thank you for your time,' said Hope. 'I'm sorry to have awakened you.' She left, closing the door on her own, and stood in the corridor for a moment. She went back down to Ross, continuing through CCTV.

'Anything else to tell me?'

'Not really, I've been watching the other floor. Movements tie in, we see Rupert going out. But we know about him now. Interestingly, of course, he didn't go anywhere near Sandra.'

'Too busy trying to sort out Angus. It's no wonder he didn't go near. Especially with her background, and what he was doing with those girls.'

Hope went and stood by the window of the hotel lobby, looking at the press cordon. She manoeuvred herself into the shade, knowing that to take an image from outside now would be difficult. As she looked at the press, she understood what Macleod had been saying.

He was there to protect her because there was a national

treasure involved. Frances had said it. You don't break the product. There's a product involved here, and the product is now dead. Well, no, Angus was now dead, but the product went on, didn't it? Plenty of people after they died still made money for people. They still had all the rights of what they'd been in. Any memoirs, things like that. You couldn't taint it.

There was every reason for this production to succeed, every reason that people wanted it to be a success. It was making money; it was doing good. So the killer had to be coming in from a different angle, maybe to bring the play down. That didn't seem to make any sense at all. After all, they were all playing roles that would benefit from the success. There had to be something else in the past.

What were they missing? Who were they missing? She went back to Ross, telling him to get back into the characters of the people who were on stage, and to cross-reference. Pull their histories and see where lives had matched and had come together. It didn't always give you the full answer. Sometimes it gave you something to go on. She would finish the CCTV. Although in truth, she didn't think it would show anything else.

Chapter 21

Macleod stood in the entrance to the theatre, awaiting the arrival of Dieter. Jona was standing beside him, with a bit of a bemused look on her face.

'You're wanting me to check this guy over. Make sure what he's saying is correct?'

'You understand the mechanics of things,' said Macleod. 'You understand how things work. I want you here just to make sure that he's telling me the truth. To make sure what he's saying is sensible.'

'Well, I'm no expert on backstage. I won't be able to tell you he's being accurate with what he's saying about how backstage works.'

'That's fine. I can deal with that. It's more to do with the technical equipment he talks about. See if what he's saying is genuine.'

'Okay,' said Jona. There was noise outside where the press had run over to a police car. Macleod watched as the constables pushed the press aside and the car trundled up to the front door of the theatre. A tall a blonde-haired man stepped out somewhere in his mid-forties with a little moustache and seemed rather bemused at the attention of the press. Once he'd stepped into the lobby of the theatre, Macleod stepped forward.

'I thank you for coming,' he said, and looked up, for Dieter was almost six foot four. He realised he towered over Jona completely.

'They said you want me to walk you around the set, to explain how everything works. I haven't been in here since that night.'

'And we have touched nothing, or rather have moved nothing significant,' said Macleod. 'I want you to go through the theatre stage and explain each piece of equipment that's backstage and around the stage. Frances Jollye said you were the one who would understand everything, it was your job to understand what each piece is.'

'It's not all ours,' said Dieter. 'Some of it is house equipment, belonging to the theatre.'

'But you know which is which?' asked Macleod.

'Yes.'

Macleod turned around to Jona and said, 'This Dieter is Miss Jona Nakamura. She's our forensic lead at Inverness and will be accompanying us. She may want to ask questions as well.'

'Fine,' said Dieter. 'Where would you like to go first?'

'Let's go onto the stage,' said Macleod. Dieter walked him up and through the hallways that led round to the stage. Walking onto the stage, he stood in the middle and turned to Macleod. 'What do you need me to do?'

'There are lots of wires, there are lighting rigs, just tell me what everything is. From the curtains to everything else.'

'Well, here you have all our marks,' said Dieter, pointing to the stage floor. We bring out our props, we set them down, but the stage is marked, so we put them in the same place each time.'

Dieter stopped for a moment. He was right beside the mark where Angus Morton had stood.

'That's Angus's mark for the last scene.'

'Yes,' said Macleod, 'we worked that one out. That's where he was when he died.'

'Yes, and Helen's is there.'

'Helen had a mark as well?'

'The last scene, she has to be in line with her gun in the story. She can't be seen to be out of position. It's the look of it. Angus was lit more than the others as well, so I have to have the right lighting.'

'And who said that had to be so?'

'Frances and me, we worked that out. That's our decision. The actors, they are told it. It's the same in every theatre. It's the last scene, so every theatre we've gone into, we've made sure that works' said Dieter. 'He also would have had on him a blood package that needs to be seen to be seeping out of his costume when he died. Obviously not real. The blood must be seen when looking at the stage, but you have to light that correctly to see blood coming through his clothing. So, we had to stand him in the correct place, to fall in the correct place, to be seen to be shot from the correct place. It's all a package,' said Dieter.

'Fine,' said Macleod, 'I understand. Please continue.'

Dieter ran through the curtains at the side, how they came across, the safety curtain that would drop, the different scenery that was available. He then moved into the wings and started showing the props and how they would be wheeled onto the stage. He pointed out trapdoors, lighting rigs, and sound equipment.

'Did you use a trapdoor?'

'No. We don't have anybody underneath. It wasn't required. You can move from one side to the other on this stage easily. So we had no one going underneath. People could move around the back, but they didn't. There was no need for it. You're usually on stage in this performance, or if you were off stage and needed to be at the other side for the next scene, you could move in between the curtain being pulled or the scenery being dropped, or we dropped the lights. There wasn't a lot of running around backstage.'

'Did anybody use it?'

'No.'

'Was it locked off?' asked Macleod.

'No.'

'So, somebody could move underneath if they wanted.'

'If they wanted, but they would be noticed. They'd be coming up on the wrong side. We all know where everybody should be.'

'Have we been underneath?' Macleod asked Jona.

'I've swept everywhere. Didn't find a gun.'

Macleod thought for a moment, then told Dieter to continue. He showed some more props in the rear and took Macleod through to where all the costumes were hanging. Jona explained she'd been through all the costumes as well. There was nothing within them. There were no remote controls, nothing to show where a gun could be stored. She was at a loss to explain what had gone on.

When they'd got through all the costumes, Dieter turned to Macleod. 'That's it,' he said. 'That's all of my stuff, everything we have brought with us.'

'What else is there?'

'Well, the rest belongs to the house.'

'Show me,' said Macleod.

Dieter ran through some smaller screens and parts. He then turned to one and said to Macleod, 'This is from the house, a support screen. It blocks out light, but we didn't use it. It's just been kept at the back. It can be very complicated. I don't like to use things like that.'

'Just stay there a moment, please,' he said to Dieter, and Macleod advised Jona to remain with Dieter while he made his way upstairs. A minimal crew of the theatre staff had been allowed access to their offices and Macleod went there to find the house manager.

'Could you come with me, sir?' he asked.

Martin Brough looked up at him. 'Of course.' He followed Macleod back down to the stage and then into backstage.

'Dieter here is taking me through and showing me all of their equipment,' said Macleod. 'He's also taking me through to show me yours. He's stopped and said that this piece of equipment—a screen of some sort—he said it's very complicated. I was wondering if you could just explain to me what it is and why it's here.'

Martin looked up at it. 'This is yours, Dieter. It's not mine.'

'No, no,' said Dieter. 'This is not mine. This is not mine at all. We didn't bring this.'

'No,' said Martin. 'This is yours. I don't have one of these.'

'Well, somebody's brought it,' said Macleod.

'I have a full list of all of our equipment. Everything's catalogued,' said Martin.

'As is mine,' said Dieter.

'Let's have both lists then,' said Macleod. He sat down in one of the stall seats of the theatre while both men were sent to bring back their records. They went through it all, and Macleod matched up every piece of equipment, and sure enough this one was on no one's inventory. Jona, meanwhile, was photographing it, and pondering it.

'So, this is nobody's,' said Macleod. 'It's not part of the theatre, and it's not part of the production company. So when did this arrive.'

'I don't remember it being here until the production company arrived,' said Martin. 'I thought it was theirs. I haven't paid it much attention.'

'It was here on that first day,' said Dieter. 'Somebody brought it in.'

Macleod stood looking at it, but it just looked like a screen. Jona, however, was showing much interest in it. She was now sitting cross-legged on the floor, looking at it. Every now and again, she would tilt her head this way and that. She then jumped up, and walked over to the area where the three holes were in the floor of the stage.

Jona picked up her phone and sent a message. She sat down again, and ten minutes later, one of her staff arrived. Together with her colleague, Jona reinserted the fixings into the holes in the stage. She then walked over to the screen again, but by now Macleod was far too intrigued.

'What are you doing?' he said.

'I photographed it, and I've taken down a description of it. Are you okay if I now handle it?'

'Have you taken any fingerprints of it?'

'I don't think we'll find any, because we did that before. We fingerprinted everywhere. We found nothing unique.'

'So we have touched this,' said Macleod.

'Yes, it was part and parcel of what we did. We went through everything. But this one, now that I look at it . . .'

'What do you mean, now that you look at it?'

'Now that I look at it, now that we look at the fixings and at the holes, the idea of a stand seems real. I think this can change, that this could be something else, that there's something within it. You have to look at it differently,' said Jona.

'So, what are you going to do?'

'Just stand clear and watch,' she said.

Macleod stepped back, and Jona seized hold of one of the poles within the framework. She spun one end of it, then spun the other, and was able to take it out. She was able to extract seven bits of polling, all of different sizes, but she screwed them together by removing some other fixings, finally able to build a sort of tripod. Jona placed it on the stage.

Macleod looked at it. 'You could put a gun on that, couldn't you?'

'You need a special type of gun, and you need it to fix in here. There's a screw that will go up into it.'

'The stand doesn't look very strong though,' said Macleod. Jona picked it up and moved over to the three holes in the floor. She was able to screw each of the legs she created into one of the holes. She turned around and kicked the structure, but it didn't move.

'Wow,' said Macleod.

'Wow indeed,' said Jona. 'Well, I guess that shows us something,' said Macleod. 'That's where it's been. Somebody—'

'Let me stop you,' said Jona. She took a deep breath. 'How long did it take you to get onto the stage?'

'Minute? A minute and a half? Maybe?'

'This has to go somewhere,' she said. 'This has to be back in position. Where is everyone? Where did they come from to fix it?'

'You mean put it away in the time frame available?'

'Time frame for being up there,' said Jona. 'You said Clarissa was on stage before to me. You and Clarissa got up. You've got a minute, a minute and a half? The actors are still on stage,' said Macleod.

'So who can deal with it?' asked Jona.

'The two from the wings. Your people,' Macleod said to Dieter.

'Peter's there,' he said, pointing off stage right. Macleod walked over and stood looking out to the stage.

'Peter was definitely there? Where's Julie?'

Dieter walked over and stood and said, 'Here.'

Macleod couldn't see Dieter. 'There?'

'Not long before, she would have been back here and she would have pushed this bit of scenery back out of the way,' said Dieter.

'In her statement, Peter and she both said they froze, unsure of what was going on. Peter said he was frightened. He was looking out.'

'What else?' asked Dieter.

'Julie said to me she was crouched and frightened. Helen said that as well.'

Macleod thought back through the statements that had been taken, and Julie had indeed said she was frightened. Helen had recorded her being there.

'Jona, go stand where Dieter is.' Jona went to where Dieter was. Macleod stepped out and took up Helen's position.

'Jona. Quick as you can, get to where the tripod is, then stop.' It took Jona less than five seconds to get around the back of the stage. Macleod made her repeat it as he stood in everybody else's position. The only person who could have seen her was Sandra, but she was looking the wrong direction. And even then, it was just a hand reaching out. A hand, but she would have had to unscrew the poles.

'How did those fixtures at the bottom work?' Macleod asked Jona. She pressed a switch and could free the tripod straightaway.

'Helen said, Julie was there. Helen said it worked. How long do they have to set that up? Would anybody see in the background?'

'You can't see,' said Dieter. 'If you're on stage, Angus has a bright light in his face. He can barely see Helen. That light would be incredibly bright. He looks off outside. He's not looking into the wings. The wings are deliberately dark,' said Dieter.

'Watch this,' said Jona. She went and stood where Julie was, and said to Macleod. 'You stand where Sandra was. Look forward. Look onto the stage.'

Macleod said, 'Go,' and started a stopwatch on his phone. Jona disappeared into the backstage, and ten seconds later when Macleod looked round, there was no tripod. Forty-five seconds had gone when Jona reappeared back at the position Julie had been in.

'What did you do?' he asked.

'Come and look at this,' she said. Macleod walked into the backstage area. There, perfectly rebuilt, looking exactly as it had done when he first arrived, was the mysterious screen that nobody would lay claim to.

'This can be done,' she said. 'This can be done. If I can do it with very little practice,' said Jona, 'they could have done it.'

'But the only person who could do it,' said Macleod, 'was Julie. Why? We have got nothing on her.'

'Julie's a decent girl,' said Dieter. 'Julie works hard, brilliant.'

'Helen would have seen her,' said Macleod. 'Helen did see her. Helen said she was there.' He paused for a moment.

'We still have the gun to think about,' Jona said.

'Jona, what happened to the gun?'

'You want me to solve everything for you?' she said. 'What I can tell you is it isn't around here.'

'Are you sure?' said Macleod.

'If it's in here, they've done a heck of a job. It'll make this screen look like nothing.'

Macleod knew he was onto something. He just couldn't quite grasp all the details. Helen had said Julie was standing in the wings. She had been there. But that had been at the start. Helen was then in shock because Angus had been shot right in front of her. He'd have gone over completely differently than if he'd simply acted it out. And she was still holding a gun.

The woman had been shaken, terrified. Afterwards, when they'd interviewed her, she was a mess. However, there was doubt about Julie. After all, Peter, the other stagehand, had said Julie had been there backstage with him. But he couldn't truly have seen her. She'd been doing what she was doing before, but he didn't have her in a line of sight and he'd probably been watching the stage.

Jona had shown that a stand could be built and had been brought in surreptitiously. So where had that come from? The only people who could have brought it in would have been the production crew or someone sneaking in from the theatre. But why the theatre crew? There was no one from the house theatre who was in any way plausible.

That being said, why would Julie want to kill him? Why

would Helen want to? There was no one except possibly Sandra, but she was dead. If she even knew about him beyond the rumours? Rupert, but he didn't seem the killing type. He just wanted everything covered up, and he hadn't moved until Angus was dead, anyway. Macleod was missing something.

His mobile vibrated in his pocket, and Macleod answered it on seeing it was Hope.

'What have you got?'

'Everyone's been in Sandra's room. The only one who's been in there for a long period was our director Frances, but she said Sandra was talking about quitting and would not go on with the production. Said that it was unusual for her because she was a trooper. She was the sort of professional who was known for continuing even when bad things happened. Frances said she found that strange. But everybody visited her in the time between her and Angus's deaths.'

'I'm in the theatre at the moment. Come back. Bring Ross, Perry and Susan in here too. We're missing something. I want to explain to you what's been going on here.'

'Will do,' said Hope.

Macleod searched for a coffee and ended up having to make one from the dispenser at the front of the Theatre. He sat down at a small table in the foyer with Hope, Perry, Susan and Ross around him.

'I've just spent time with Jona, and we've proved that a stand is actually in there.'

'A what?' said Hope.

'There's a screen in there that you can take the parts off and build a stand that goes straight into the floor. Jona proved it can be dismantled and put back into place in under a minute. It could have been removed, put back to look like a screen in under a minute during the time I was rushing to get up to the stage.'

'So, somebody backstage did it. All the actors are on the stage, though,' said Hope.

'So there is somebody there,' said Macleod, 'that we don't know about or our stagehands are prime suspects.'

'But they said they saw each other. Are they in collusion?'

'Peter in his position can't see Julie,' said Macleod. 'I went through it. Now, she might have been there doing things just beforehand, but he's watching the scene, of course, as it happens. She's out of his view. She's also out of view if she moves from where she was to sort out this stand. But I've got nothing against her, nothing to say about why she would do it. We also haven't got a gun there. The gun isn't hidden inside something. The gun has been put somewhere.'

'It's also got to be fired,' said Perry. 'How did they fire it? We were talking about it being automated. Or have we got somebody else there?'

'It must be automated,' said Hope. 'You don't go to the bother of building a stand to fire it yourself. Why? Why not just hold it?'

'Because the line of sight has to be right,' said Perry. 'Sorry, but it doesn't rule out an extra person being back there.'

'We're almost there,' said Macleod. 'We must be almost there.'

'Well, the evidence shows the only one capable of handling a gun is going to be Frances, the director. Either that or Sandra did it, but why would Sandra do it? And she couldn't anyway. She was on the stage,' said Hope.

'Well, it can't be Frances,' said Macleod. 'Frances is at the back of the theatre. She's down below the sound and lighting decks. She can't get there, can't do it in time.'

'What happened after you got on the stage, though?' asked Hope. 'You got on the stage, but people are still milling about. They're still running around, aren't they, after that?'

'They're on the stage until I get on there. Then we start looking and hunting. The only concern, of course, has us looking down. Clarissa's gone, searching around for someone. The stand's already gone at that point,' said Macleod.

'So, somebody goes, breaks the stand down, and has the gun. That's the time when the gun gets moved. It gets put somewhere else,' said Perry.

'But where?' said Macleod. 'Where?'

'Maybe we need to see who triggered it,' said Hope. 'If we knew who triggered it, then we might have a better line of attack. We might not get this on motive. We might have to get this on opportunity, first.'

'Well, everyone's standing,' said Macleod, 'in position when the shot goes out.' He sat for a moment, thinking. 'Hands,' he said. 'People's hands. You'd have to activate it with your hand, wouldn't you?'

'Presume so,' said Hope. 'We're not going to go into thought processes, are we? You will not have something wired up inside your teeth so you can crunch on it.'

'Or you could think of the foot,' said Perry.

'On your foot,' said Ross. 'You can activate that too easily.'

'Who can't we see? Peter? Julie? Peter could activate it. They're having to watch, aren't they? Julie could activate it.'

'But where's she carrying it?' asked Macleod. 'And what do they do to get rid of it? People at the back of the stage—they wear little. They're in black. Simple clothing. Not clanking around with things.'

'What if it's a team?' said Susan suddenly. 'One setting it off.

The other one is tidying up.'

'What do you mean?' asked Macleod.

'Think about it,' said Susan. 'There's a lot going on. But somebody has to take that shot. Who knows when they're in the right place? Who knows when he's made his mark? Who can see that the easiest?'

'Helen,' said Perry. 'She's closest to him. And she knows he's going to be in the right mark because she's firing a fake gun at him.'

'She's also very close,' said Hope, 'though. The line of the shot. It's very close to Helen.'

'All the more reason,' said Perry. 'You want to control that shot. You don't want to be half stumbling and somebody else lets it go and kills you. You want to be in charge of it.'

'But,' said Macleod, 'we still don't know why Helen wants to kill him.' He stopped for a moment. 'I hate to say it,' he said. 'I'm going to need Clarissa's help.'

Ross raised an eyebrow, but Macleod picked up his phone and dialled Clarissa, then left it on speaker, sitting on the table.

'What's up?' asked Clarissa. 'Saw you were on the news, but said you had made little progress.'

'Listen,' said Macleod. 'Take a moment over this. I need you to think back to the night when it happened. When they shot Angus Morton, you and I were watching the stage. I want you to tell me what you saw. Any motion. You were on a different side of the theatre from me.'

'What am I meant to be looking for? I told you where everybody was. I told you what they were doing. They were all acting.'

'Think,' said Macleod. 'They're all looking at him. Yes.'

'Yes,' said Clarissa.

'What are they doing with their hands?' said Macleod.

'Don't know about Sandra. Couldn't see hers. I can see Helen. I can see Angus. Can't see anybody in the back. Rupert's hands were clear at that time. He's holding them out.'

'Yes, he was,' said Macleod. 'Alistair's looked relaxed. Also, a little out. She's raised a gun , so he's putting his hands up to tell everybody to stop.'

'Yes, Helen had one hand on the gun, but her other hand…,' said Clarissa. 'Hang on a minute. Her other hand, it was tight by her side. It actually was gripping her dress. I remember thinking it didn't quite feel right, but I reckoned they were just trying to make it tense-looking.'

'What do you mean she was gripping?' asked Macleod.

'Holding it tight, squeezing it. It was bunched up.'

Macleod looked across at Hope. 'Go find the outfit she was wearing. Check it. Check it for hidden pockets. Check it in case it's still got a device in it.'

Hope disappeared from the table and Susan headed after her.

'What happened to her hand after that?'

'She unbunched. He was shot. I think she let the grasp go. She did!' said Clarissa.

'It's unusual, isn't it? You would have gripped tighter. You would panic. Your reflex would be to grip your hands together, not to throw them apart.'

'Totally. She was also still afterwards.'

'Like she'd been holding herself in place. Like,' said Macleod, 'she was tensed because she knew a bullet was coming past her.'

'When you put it that way, when you look at it in that context, it's a possibility, Seoras,' said Clarissa.

Macleod stood up and paced. 'So why? Why are they doing it? Come on, Ross. Why are they doing it? What's in the background?'

'Underage,' said Macleod. 'Underage. Look into that again. Go back into that. Cross-reference to where they all are. Just get back into it, Ross. It's got to be in there somewhere.'

Ross disappeared, and Macleod looked at Perry. 'Where's the gun gone? What do they do with the gun?'

'Give it away. Got to get it out of there,' said Perry.

Macleod sat and thought for a moment. 'How do you get it away? What do you get it out of the way in? What do you…,'

'What happened afterwards?' asked Perry.

'I checked the gun on stage. It was clear it wasn't capable of firing. So where did the prop go after that?'

'I don't know, but they're wandering around with a gun. They're wandering with a gun. You can't just walk it out of there. It hasn't been left behind. It has to be…?'

The two men sat looking at each other, and then Hope came back.

'The dress, there's a pouch in it. It's small enough to fit something into it. It's around that area where Helen would have grabbed. There seems to be no reason for it. I'm no clothes maker, but there doesn't seem to be a reason for it to be there. It looks reasonable that they could have had something in there, then slip it away afterwards.'

'They've got plenty of opportunities. People are slipping here, there and wherever. So where is it? Where has it gone?'

Macleod sat looking at Perry. 'I checked that gun. I checked Helen's gun and then it was taken away from her. Taken away from there.' *By who?* thought Macleod. 'Initially, it was taken because I checked it. It wasn't real. Couldn't have fired. It didn't fire. Its trajectory was all wrong, anyway.'

'I assume the props person would have taken it,' said Perry. 'No one else would have known where to put it, and why would anybody else take it off her. They would just leave it there. A props person would have put it away. If they took it, you wouldn't have thought twice about it, would you?'

'I was watching,' said Macleod, 'I was watching what was happening with Angus. I was trying to see if he could be revived, trying to make sure everybody was okay, and then— Jane was there, Jane was there, I wonder did she see it?'

Macleod picked up his phone again and dialled Jane.

'Yeah, what's up? You haven't finished it, have you?'

'No, no, I'm on the case. Think for me, think for me.'

'Think what, Seoras?'

'When you came up to the stage, and you said, "Is there anything I can do?" And I said, "Just keep everybody back off the stage," do you remember the gun? The fake gun?'

'Yes. But you picked that up. You had a look at it. There was a fake gun.'

'What happened to it afterwards?'

'Girl at the back took it. That's what happened.'

'And what did she do with it?' asked Macleod.

Macleod turned around to Perry. 'Where was that gun when Jona had it? Do you remember?'

Perry picked up his mobile and called Jona. It took her a few moments before she told him.

'Jona says when they first found it, the gun was outside the ladies' toilets.'

'What was it doing outside the ladies' toilets?' asked Macleod. Perry went back on the phone.

'There were boxes and props set there. Apparently, that's

where it should have been.'

'Let's go to the ladies' toilets,' said Macleod to Hope. Macleod followed her as Hope burst into the ladies' toilets. There was nobody there. Macleod noted the different cubicles.

'What are you looking for?' asked Hope.

'Window. There's no window here, Hope. Why is there no window?'

He looked around him. 'You have to get a gun out of here. Therefore, if you brought it into the ladies' toilets and you could get it here without being discovered, you would just pass it out the window. Maybe somebody outside the window could get it.'

'Clarissa was at the perimeter. We went through all of that. There was nobody.'

'Did they flush it?' asked Macleod.

'Can't flush it,' said Hope. 'What if it gets stuck? Look at those toilets down there. How does it get out and around the pipe? And they don't want it found, do they? Because if it gets found, they can trace the bullet. They can say that's the gun that did it. They can—'

'So, you don't. You could throw it into the sanitary bins.'

Hope began pulling open the bins, delving into them. 'These haven't been emptied since. Well, nobody's been in to do it,' she said. There was no heaviness in any of the bins. Wading through the discarded towels and packages, Hope couldn't find anything.

'Somewhere else.'

Macleod looked at the tops of all the toilets. He stepped forward and lifted off the lid of the cistern. He looked down into the first toilet. There was a little bricklike object sitting inside it.

'What's this?' asked Macleod.

'That's just one of those toilet bricks,' said Hope.

Macleod reached in, lifted it out, and it was indeed a toilet brick. There was no opening, just a heavy brick. He went into the next one and lifted it up. It too had the same. And also in the third cubicle. 'We're stretching it,' said Hope.

Macleod ignored her. He took off the lid of the next cistern and reached down. This brick looked similar. But when he touched it, even through the water, it had more of a plastic feel about it. He took it up. Gripping it, Macleod cracked open the brick, and a gun was inside. Hope nodded to Perry, who picked up his phone, calling Jona.

'So, somebody's brought it here,' said Hope.

'And I know how,' said Macleod. He stepped out of the women's toilets, looked and saw the prop gun, the one that Helen had been holding. Pulling at it, the prop came apart into two, the middle of it being empty. He brought it back inside the toilets and placed it down beside the real gun.

'I thought it looked large,' he said, 'but there's no weight to it. It's been stuffed in here, brought to these toilets, dumped, and then the fake weapon is put here. I even checked the prop before they used it to transport the real gun.'

'So we're saying what?' said Hope. 'Helen fired the gun remotely?'

'And Julie put the stand there and put the gun on it, ready to be fired. And then Julie got it away. Helen's attracted all the attention. She's known the whole time. She just acted out her suffering. Clever.'

'Then we need to find them,' said Hope.

Hope and Macleod raced out of the building, telling Perry to wait for Jona before following. Hope drove the car quickly around to the hotel, where Macleod ignored the press that came racing towards him, telling the constables to keep them back. Once inside, he raced up to her room, but Helen wasn't there.

He raced back down, and the concierge told him she'd left. Julie was gone too. Macleod raced back up to the room with the hotel staff, who opened the door for him, and Macleod stepped inside. He looked around quickly, but there were no signs of distress. No signs of anything. *Where could they have gone?* thought Macleod.

He was worried now. Less about them disappearing, and more about their own safety. *Why had they run?* As he looked around the room, he noticed the cups were different on this level from the floor above. The rooms were different too. The cups were more basic, with posher ones on the floor above. Hope came into the room, having been in Julie's room.

'No sign of her either. All her stuff's still here.'

'Then what are they doing?' asked Macleod. 'Have they run? Have they panicked?' He gripped his hands together. He was so close but needed to piece the last parts together.

Chapter 23

Macleod was frustrated. He was so close. So very close. But he didn't have proof of anything. Jona was working on the gun. They'd be able to match the bullet to it. But he had no device that would automate the gun. Where had it gone? It might have been small. They could have walked out with it, of course.

People weren't strip-searched before they left the building. They were looking for guns, not for something small. Would they even recognise it? If Julie had made it, it could have looked like anything. After all, that's what she did. But there was another strand missing here.

Macleod called the hotel housekeeping staff to him. The supervisor stepped forward, and Macleod explained what he wanted them to do.

'There's a cup upstairs that's come from this floor,' he said. 'I want you to check these rooms and see if there're any cups missing. They'll need to be replaced.'

The supervisor thought it an easy enough request and sent off his team to have a look in the various rooms. The supervisor came back only ten minutes later.

'All the cups at the moment are accounted for. However,

we had a room the other day where a cup was missing. We record these things, just so it shows we aren't taking them. It helps the company, claim for breakages, damage, etc. It helps monitor what they go through.'

'And when? When did this happen? And which room?' urged Macleod.

'It was a few days ago. Two days ago, I think,' said the man. The man checked his list. 'And the room where it occurred was that of Miss Julie Flip.'

Macleod grabbed Hope, asking to take him back down to the CCTV. They watched the images of Julie going back and forward to Sandra's. She did it only twice, but one time, Macleod was convinced he could see white in her hands. The image was never the best, but something was there.

'Has she taken the cup one time, swapped it, and then come back?'

'Well, she's not realised that if you swap the cup, it'll be different,' said Macleod.

'Either that,' said Hope, 'or she knows it's good to be different because she knows what's got the poison in it.'

Perry approached Macleod while he was watching the CCTV.

'We can't find them. Staff said they disappeared from the hotel; they just left, gone in a taxi. I've traced that taxi, but it's gone cold as well. Maybe they've got a car somewhere, but I can't find them at the moment.'

'Well, we need to chase it; we need to find out where they've gone because I still think there's more to come.'

'In what way?'

'Somebody put them up to this,' said Macleod, 'somebody is going to get them out of it. They've gone and left everything, they've taken nothing with them. That's a new life they're headed to; that's something different; that's an escape plan.'

'But who?' asked Perry.

'Whoever provided the gun. These two didn't get hold of a gun. These two didn't know what they were doing with it. Somebody would have had to train them up, what to expect with the gun, what to do with it. Somebody else wanted Angus dead as well as these two.'

Macleod pulled in everyone else in the troupe from Frances to Dieter, Peter and Alistair. They all said they were shocked that the woman had gone, and couldn't think of why they'd disappeared.

'When was the last you spoke to them?'

'I haven't,' said Frances. 'To be honest, I don't feel safe around anyone, so I've been keeping out of it, staying in my room. Your police constables will tell you that. I haven't moved.'

'I've not gone far either,' said Alistair.

'Well, I saw the girls at dinner. I was just eating. They were eating separately, and they came over. Asked me about why I'd been taken away by you,' said Dieter.

'What did you say?'

'I told them about finding the stand.'

'The girls could be in trouble,' said Hope to Macleod on hearing this.

'Because,' said Macleod, 'they're a link. If they know we've found out how they've done it, and the girls will go down for it, they may be on an escape plan. They'll look to protect the women. Or somebody, especially if they're into gun running, is going to close off all links, make sure they can't be traced, make sure the deaths don't come back to them. It's one way or the other, isn't it?'

'Well, let's get out there,' said Hope. 'Let's find out where they've gone, see what we can do. The taxi, that picked them up, trace that taxi. If it's a train, if it's the bus, anywhere. We're going to have to start a manhunt.'

Macleod felt his phone vibrating and picked it up to see Ross indicated on the screen.

'Sir, I've been doing a bit more digging.'

'You'd better make it quick, Ross. We're chasing the girls. I'm going to need you involved in the manhunt too.'

'Listen,' said Ross. 'You said to look for the underage link. I think I've found it. I started looking connections between the troupe and sex rings. So, I looked for any time anybody in the troop is mentioned in regards to a sex ring or close to it. Outside of Angus, there's very little. Except once.'

'Who?' asked Macleod.

'Helen.'

'Helen? What's Helen got to do with a sex ring?'

'Nothing, but she's been on a satellite channel doing a documentary.'

'What?' said Macleod.

'She's done a documentary. I've got it here.'

'I am there in ten minutes,' said Macleod. 'Get it ready for me.'

Macleod turned, found Perry, explained the situation and then bolted out the door. He jumped in the back of a police car and whizzed through the press cordon. They all seemed desperately excited to see him in action. Arriving back at the station, Macleod tore up the stairs, finding himself out of breath as he reached the office of the murder team.

'Sit,' said Ross. Macleod took up a chair behind Ross's desk, and in front of him a documentary was playing. It was a satellite documentary on a small channel. Macleod could see Helen. She was young and pretty, almost pouting in front of the camera. It was quite classless, and for the first couple of minutes, it seemed to be quite bombastic and over the top, but then Macleod saw her interview someone that he knew.

Jameson senior was there explaining how he hated those who would prey on underage girls. Helen was taken into the clubs of the Jamesons and with careful camera shots, it could be seen the girls who were working in the strip joints were dancing provocatively. Any body parts were covered with a fuzzy screen. However, Jameson pointed out and showed documentation that every girl up there was over eighteen.

Macleod remembered the conversation. *Jameson senior had been disgusted. He'd thrown him out. He'd got rid of Angus. So, what had changed? Why hadn't he got rid of him earlier? Why hadn't he?* He sat back in the chair for a moment before turning to Ross.

'Yes, sir?' said Ross.

'You've got Helen and you've got Julie. Now, it looks like they've set up this killing. I've now got Helen talking to Jameson. When I spoke to Jameson down in Glasgow, he was adamant that all his girls were of a legal age and that he hated those who went with underage girls.'

'Well, that's not uncommon. There are standards among criminals.'

'Yes, yes, there are, Ross. But,' said Macleod, 'he also did nothing to Angus Morton because he said he was so big, he just got rid of him from his clubs. He was quite happy to gamble with him, but as soon as he found this out, this side of him, he got rid of him. He didn't want Morton anywhere near him. But he did nothing physical, because the connection had been made to Jameson. They were gambling together. If Angus Morton had died there and then, in the aftermath of throwing him out, there would have been talk of owing money, all the rest of it, and an investigation. Jameson needed to be clear. But then, how has he got the girls to do this?'

'You don't think the girls might have experienced something?' said Ross. 'Maybe they're victims.'

'Well, we're not going to find out, are we?' said Macleod. 'Not until it all comes out in the wash, because Angus Morton was never convicted of anything. He was never proven to be in the company of young girls. Never proved to have done anything illegal.'

Macleod sat, his chin on his hand. 'If we're quick,' he said. 'If we're quick, we might just be able to catch them all.'

'Sir?' asked Ross.

'Jameson will not kill them. He got them the gun. Jameson is trying to get them out. He's going to send them away, going to put them in a different country, do something like that. They know it's blown now. Julie's gone for help. But there's going to be a time and a place to meet, and it won't be in Inverness. They're on the move to somewhere to get picked up.'

Macleod picked up his phone and called Glasgow. He spoke to one of the crime officers down there, a detective chief inspector, asking him for the movements of Jameson, both senior and junior. They hadn't been seen for a good twenty-four hours.

Macleod thumped the desk. Jameson had stood in front of him. Jameson said to him as much. The man was this close to turning around and telling Macleod, telling him Morton deserved it. In fact, he'd said that. He'd said good luck to those who would do it. He said—Macleod stood up.

'Find them for me, Ross. Find them for me,' he said. 'We need to get them quickly.' Ross nodded and gently pushed Macleod's chair away from his desk, slipping in behind the computer. Soon Hope was on the phone and Ross, along with Hope, was coordinating a manhunt.

Macleod walked over to Hope's office and sat down in her chair. He spun around and looked out of the window. It was one of those times. He'd played the pieces. He'd made the move, he'd got the connections, now he was playing the pieces. If he knew where to go, he'd go. He needed the team to find out where. There was nobody for him to interview. Not anymore.

Sandra must have found out. Must have seen something. That's why she was dead. Jameson would have done that. Would have encouraged them. *He's not going to kill the girls*, he thought. *He's going to get them away.*

Macleod looked over and saw Ross working away. The rest of his team would be out there, scrambling about, trying to find any connection to how the girls had moved on from the hotel.

And here he was. About to stand and look out the window. *Oh well*, he thought, *should make myself useful.* He moseyed through into the office and refilled the filter machine and waited for the coffee to be produced. When he'd done that, he poured a cup and placed it in front of Ross.

'Thank you, sir.'

'It's Seoras,' he said. 'Would you just call me Seoras? It won't be sir for much longer.'

'Yes, sir,' said Ross. Macleod took his own coffee and went back into Hope's office. He would have to wait, and he didn't like it. So, he picked up the phone and called Jane.

'How are you getting on?' she asked.

'Nearly there, I'm nearly finished.'

'They said on the news you've got nowhere.'

'You know better than to listen to the news,' said Macleod.

'Will I see you tonight?'

'I hope so,' said Macleod, 'I really hope so, but if not, the one after that, and probably the one after that too.'

'What's up?' asked Jane.

'I'm almost there,' said Macleod, 'but there's something within me that almost doesn't want to catch them this time.'

'It's time you retired,' said Jane.

'Yes, it is. I'll ring you when I'm done.' He put down the phone and looked over at Ross, working hard behind his laptop. *Come on*, he thought. *Nearly there. Come on!*

Chapter 24

ope arrived at the hotel alongside Perry and Susan and made a beeline straight for the reception.

'Can I help?' said the concierge.

'The two women from the theatre, Helen Love and Julie Flip, we were told they left together.'

'That's correct. In fact, they came and asked for a taxi.'

'Which firm was it?'

'Here,' he said. 'This one we always use,' and handed over a card. *One, two, three taxis*, thought Hope. They were a small firm in Inverness, band she immediately pulled out her phone, contacting them.

'This is Detective Inspector Hope McGrath. I'm looking for some information about a hire you took recently.' She gave the name of the hotel and then waited while the woman scanned the inputs on her computer.

'Oh, Davey did that one.'

'Do you know where he is at the moment?'

'He's on a job; do you want me to get him to you?'

'Absolutely,' said Hope, 'as soon as you can.'

'Just give me a moment.'

'He'll be with you in about ten minutes,' said the woman. 'If you just stay at the hotel, he'll come to you.'

'Did the computer say where he was going, where the fare was for?'

'No, and it's not come up in the system yet. He won't be hiding it; it'll just be, it hasn't filtered in. If they don't give it when they call in initially, and if it's from the hotel, we don't always know.'

'Okay,' she said. Hope turned and explained the situation to Perry and Susan, and then strode out into the car park. There was a line of press as usual, several of them calling her over, looking for a statement. Hope ignored them, scanning beyond them, and after ten minutes saw a taxi pulling in.

'Let that one through,' said Hope. The taxi drove up, and the taxi driver went to get out, but Hope indicated for him to leave the doors open and got into his passenger seat.

'I believe you picked up two women here recently. Actress and her friend.'

'I don't know who they are, but yes, I did,' said the man.

'Where'd you take them?'

'Dropped them in town, at this location,' said the man, pulling out his phone and pulling up the maps. 'It was just around the corner from John's former hire car firm.'

'Did they indicate where they were going?'

'Didn't say a word, paid cash,' said the man. 'Went to give them a receipt, but they didn't take it.'

'Anything else?'

'Had a small bag with them,' the man said. 'Not much to it though.'

'Thank you,' said Hope. She stepped out of the car and made for Perry and Susan. 'They got dropped here, just beyond John's former car rental. Get down there, check out the car hire firm, anything else around there. I'm going to talk to Ross.'

Hope picked up the phone, called Ross, advising him where the two women had got out of the taxi.

'Could make for the bus from there or a train, not that far to walk back into town and pick the train up.'

'No, it's not,' said Hope.

'It's obvious though, isn't it?'

'Well, not everybody's been on the run before,' said Hope. 'Maybe they don't know what they're doing.'

'They're trying to get somewhere. They don't have a car with them. I doubt they'll have false IDs as well. How do you get somewhere? If you go by train or by bus, it takes you time. You're also on CCTV. If they're making a run for it, this might be their idea of how they do it.'

'They'll be being picked up somewhere then,' said Hope. 'We need to find them before that.'

'I doubt it will be in Inverness,' said Ross. 'I'll start looking.'

* * *

Susan halted the car outside the front door of the car hire firm and Perry jumped out. He marched to the front desk, holding his credentials up.

'Sorry to bother you, it's Detective Constable Warren Perry. I need to speak to you urgently. Have you had two women recently come in, or a single woman, trying to hire a car under the names of Helen Love or Julie Flip?'

'Flip,' said the woman. 'Flip rings the bell. Hang on.' She went behind her computer, tapped in a few numbers, and then looked up at Perry. 'Yes. She's gone maybe twenty-five minutes, half an hour ago.'

'What car did they take?'

'It was a red Ford Fiesta.'

'License plate?' The woman quoted it, and Perry made a note. 'Did they say anything about where they were going or when they were going to return the car?'

'Said they'd be returning the car in three days' time.'

'Thank you,' said Perry. He picked up his phone as he headed back to the car. As he sat in the passenger seat, Susan looked across at him. 'Got them,' he said, but the phone had already connected through to Ross. 'Ross, here's the licence plate. You're looking for a red Ford Fiesta.'

'I'll get on it,' said Ross. 'I'll put out a message for all the local cars as well and check the car flow cameras.'

'They said three days for a return. I think they're heading straight down the A9,' said Perry. 'If Macleod thinks they're going to meet with people like Jameson, and he's going to be coming up from Glasgow, they will not go north and pick them up. This is going to be quick.'

'Indeed,' said Ross, 'but they've got to get up from Glasgow. Somebody might have to wait around for a while. I'll get on it.'

Perry called Hope, updating her on the situation and explaining what Ross was doing. Having closed down the call, Susan turned to Perry. 'Where do we go now?'

'We don't go anywhere,' said Perry. 'Nowhere to go. They've left here. They're in a car. We've got to spot them first. I think they'll be heading to Glasgow, but we don't know. I say we get ourselves some food. We may not see something else to eat for a while.'

Susan nodded and pulled out, heading for a local fast-food stop.

* * *

The door of Hope's office opened, and Macleod spun in her chair.

'You planning on taking up residence in here again? You've got an office of your own.'

'Anything?' asked Macleod.

'Got the car they're off in. Got everybody out looking for it. It's a trawl now. Ross has got a watch out on their credit cards too, but they'll probably not be that daft.'

'They were daft enough to take a taxi,' said Macleod.

'But they're being quick. Now they're in a hire car.'

'I would have stolen one,' said Macleod. 'That would have been easier.'

'They go on the train, they're trapped. They go on the bus, people will see them. This way, they can drive and hide until it's time for their rendezvous.'

'Jamesons will be coming up from Glasgow,' said Macleod. 'That's who they'll be meeting. Glasgow have said they can't find them.'

'So, they're already on the move,' said Hope. 'We better find this car quick.'

Macleod stood up and turned. He looked out the window. 'I still miss this, you know. It's a great comfort being able to look out here, and you've got everything in motion.'

'If I get a call about this car, are you coming with me?'

'Of course,' said Macleod. He didn't turn around, but he could hear Hope fidgeting.

'Am I in the way?' he said. 'Do you want me to…?'

'No,' she said. 'It's just you're down here. You're . . .'

'This will be the last one,' said Macleod. 'This will be it. These have been my last times looking out of this window, certainly on a job. You don't know how often I've stood here. This has been life; this has been what I've done. In the next couple of days, that will be it. We'll be winding up. You'll be able to wrap it up. I'll come back as you need me, make statements, tie up the processes, but they will only be visits in. I won't be working, so to speak, won't be on the chase, won't be on the deduction side of it. This is it. I'm chasing after two women who killed a man we now believe was into underage girls. It's hardly the most glorious finish, is it?'

'You don't get to pick,' said Hope. 'We get our cases. You brought down the Forseti group.'

'I can look back on a lot of them,' said Macleod. 'But look back on what? Murder, death. Jane says I shouldn't look back at all.'

'You've done a lot of good things, though,' said Hope. 'I'm here.'

He turned and looked at her. 'You are here, and look at you too. More than ready. You could take the DCI role if they offered it to you. And I think they might.'

'Don't they have your replacement lined up?'

'No,' he said.

'I thought you were just holding out on me.'

'They'll offer it to you. You look good as a DCI. Young, dynamic woman. You could do the job, but I wouldn't take it.'

'Why?' asked Hope.

'Because then you'd be out of here and have to start managing people. You're not a manager. You're a detective. When you get old like me, you can do the managing bit for a while. But then you'll have somebody to bring on, to step into your shoes if you step out of here. Look at your team. Who do you want to bring on? You'd also be in charge of Clarissa, God help you. You'd also be in charge of Emmett. He's different. You don't want that. You want to be here in the cut and thrust.'

'You remember this with fondness,' said Hope.

'I'll remember you all with fondness. It's very hard to remember looking at dead bodies with fondness. But I have pride in the job, or I did. And I got most of them right, I think.'

Her desk phone rang. Macleod went to reach for it and then stopped. He looked at Hope, but she nodded. Macleod picked up the phone . 'Macleod here.'

'We've got him,' said Ross. 'Heading to the Cairngorms. Tracking at the moment. Already got Perry and Susan on the way.'

'We're following. Keep us updated. We're on the mobile.'

Hope turned and grabbed her jacket, Macleod grabbing his. He tore down the steps, following Hope, and got into the car. She thought as she raced out of the car park, she saw him give a sentimental look back at the building.

As they raced down the A9, Macleod took a call. 'They've gone to a quiet car park,' said Ross. 'I've got CCTV, road cameras on the road in and the road out.'

'Well, that's pretty amateurish.'

'I don't know how well the Jamesons will know up there. I guess they're thinking they're out in the wild.'

'We need to get eyes on the car park, but quiet eyes. How far is Perry out?'

'Twenty, thirty minutes.'

'Just make sure they don't leave that car park,' said Macleod. 'I want Perry to get close.'

Macleod called Perry, told him to get eyes on the car park but not to be near it with his own car. By the time Macleod arrived, stopping a half mile away, Perry was already in position.

Macleod left Hope in the car, and walked through the undergrowth and the few trees that there were, and found Perry lying on his front. His binoculars were pointing at the car park. The night was getting dark now. Macleod could hear his stomach rumble. Perry, however, had some cold chips beside him. Macleod reached into the bag, almost startling Perry.

'They're waiting.'

'Any indication of anyone else?' asked Macleod.

'No. Susan's parked half a mile away. There's only one road in and one road out.'

'Which one have you got?' asked Macleod. Perry pointed to the far side of the car park.

'Good. Hope's on this side. I take it Susan's parked well off the road.'

'Of course.'

Macleod had only been there five minutes when his phone buzzed. Ross had sent a message. A car had passed on the way to the car park, caught on the last CCTV screen. Macleod texted Hope, and then Susan, telling them to head to the car park. It wasn't long before a car pulled up, and the women stepped out.

Macleod could see Jameson senior walking over to the girls. Helen Love was in tears, running to him, and he embraced her before telling her to get into the car. Julie Flip was a bit more circumspect, turning back to look at the car behind her, and then simply shaking Jameson's hand. Macleod looked at the car Jameson had come in and saw his son sitting in the front seat.

Macleod stood up and walked out of the undergrowth,

emerging from some trees. He held his identification up in one hand. 'I wouldn't go any further. Get your son to switch off the engine,' he said.

He heard Jameson swear, but the engine was soon cut. 'What mistake did they make?' asked Jameson.

'They left in a taxi,' said Macleod. 'Should have walked out. Should have stolen a car. Should have—'

'They were too panicked. I thought we had time. I didn't think you were there yet. Didn't think you'd—'

'I was most of the way there. I had a good idea. Found the stand. Found the gun in the toilet brick,' said Macleod.

'Was going to get that once you'd all left. Had a cleaner lined up to bring the gun back,' said Jameson.

'It was you that gave it away though,' said Macleod. 'These two, they couldn't have done it on their own. There's no way they'd get a weapon to run something that sophisticated. Julie there, once the idea's in her mind, she could work out how to do it. She could work out the subterfuge within the theatre. But you, Jameson, you would have waited.'

'He deserved it. I looked at what he was doing. They covered it up. The people who made money out of him, they covered it up.'

'I promise,' said Macleod, 'that will be investigated.'

'He deserved it,' said Jameson. 'I couldn't stand back. He deserved it. I might be a criminal but I'm not like that. He's not a man to be lauded, to be held up.'

'Why these two?' asked Macleod. 'They obviously had a reason.'

'They're close. Very close. Partners. Though they don't tell anyone,' said Jameson. 'But Helen there was one of his victims. She was a lot younger then. I found out and got in contact.

Worked it all out. Got her the role because she had a figure, they said. That wasn't why she got the role. I made sure she got the role. I made sure Julie was in there as well. Inverness was the right place. We could do more there.

'Easier to work it, and it would have been textbook, but you were watching the show. You and that rottweiler of yours. Changed everything. People didn't run screaming, people weren't causing as much mayhem. Julie couldn't work things out as quickly and then Sandra saw her. Sandra saw her with the toy gun, the prop.

'The thing was, we put the real gun inside that. Then she took it to the bathroom, and from there, she put it in the brick. It all would have been clean. You see, you would have thought somebody would have got away. Somebody would have run out of the building. But your rottweiler was too good. You screwed it up, Macleod. These two would have gone on. He would have got his comeuppance.'

'Nobody would have known,' said Macleod.

'I'd have leaked it out,' said Jameson. 'I'd have made sure his legacy was out there. Others would have been dealt with under the law. We'd have fed the information.'

A car pulled in and Hope stepped out, blocking the entrance to the car park. Susan pulled up soon after.

'We'll be taking them all in,' said Macleod, as police cars started to arrive as well.

'You do agree with me, don't you, Macleod?' said Jameson. 'He deserved it. It would have been textbook, it would have been poetic justice to have got the bastard like that. He deserved it.'

Macleod looked at Jameson and nodded. 'Without a shadow of a doubt, I found it hard to feel remorse for him.'

He saw Hope look at him. Macleod shook his shoulders. 'But the thing is, Jameson, Sandra didn't deserve any of that. She didn't deserve to die. You've made these girls into murderers, not once, but twice. The first one you could understand, especially for what he did to Helen. But Sandra deserved nothing of the sort. Wrong place, wrong time. She actually fought to give girls a better place in the theatre, against people like him.

'You should have tried going to her. She might have shut up. She was talking about leaving and not going on with the tour. That's the thing, though. You've taken those girls, traumatised as they are, and turned them into killers. That's what I can't forgive you for, what I can't accept. That's why I'll put you behind bars and throw away the key with joy. Take him, Hope.'

It was about another ten minutes before the car park was clear. Macleod said he would wait for Jona to come and do the business with the cars that were left. A couple of police cars sat on the edge of the car park. Soon it was just Hope and Macleod there waiting for Jona.

'That's that, then,' said Hope.

'Yes,' said Macleod.

'We'll need to do a press conference. Tell them. Tell them what we've discovered. Or at least as much as we can.'

'You tell them. I just want to go home. I'm done. This is just mopping up.'

'You want me to tell them? Tell them that their national hero is a sex pest. A man who did the deed with underage girls.'

'You're right,' said Macleod. 'You mop it up, I'll do the press, then I'm going home.'

'And then you're coming back,' said Hope, 'you're not leaving like this. We won. You told me once you have to celebrate, not for yourself, but for everybody else, and this lot need to say goodbye.'

'You're right,' he said, 'but tonight I'm going home to Jane, and she's coming to this next party. She needs to say goodbye too.' He looked up, and he saw a tear in Hope's eye. 'What's that for?' he said.

'Because my friend's going,' said Hope. 'The friend I never thought I'd have, not when I first saw you.' She squeezed his hand. 'Where's Jona?' she said. 'She needs to get here before I fall apart.' She walked off to talk to the other police officers in their cars, leaving Macleod on his own.

He sighed. *At least we won*, he thought. *At least we won.*

Chapter 25

The party had been something else. Half the station was there, at least everybody who didn't have to be on duty. And they'd presented Macleod with a new hat. It was a fedora. Brand new and he thought he might wear it. He needed to hang up the shirt and tie. That's what Jane had said. No more ties.

The fedora would be good. The old one he had could go. He'd cleared out his locker earlier on in the day, finally cleared the desk. He'd been in a few times, sorting out bits and pieces of the last case. But Hope had run with it now.

Jane had watched him carefully. He hadn't known how he would feel. This was it after all. This had been his life. He'd immersed himself in it after his first wife had died, and he was good at it. That was the hard bit. He knew he was good at it. Would he be good at the next stage of his life?

Jane had pointed out that he could have his morning coffee. But he missed his coffee with the team. They'd been through so much together and they'd all had words to say telling the rest of the police force about him. Telling how good he was.

His superiors had talked about how he'd led the place, brushed over the time when they'd taken him off a case. He'd had to go on his own and solve it without being a proper policeman. Macleod didn't mention that.

He'd given a few words. He told them all that he was looking forward to his life with Jane. And that was true. That was incredibly true. She deserved it. He deserved it. His joints had not been kind to him. He found it harder to get up when he was knocked down. The chase, well, it still caught him. The thrill still went through his veins but the body didn't feel the drive.

John had been there with little Ian, Hope's wee one. Macleod had held him for quite a time. He'd felt like a granddad when this one was born and Hope treated him like he was granddad. Jane had caught him staring at Hope during the night and he told Jane he just couldn't believe the change from the first time she'd worked with him. Jane said she couldn't believe the change either.

He'd done karaoke with Clarissa again. They'd murdered some songs. Clarissa had knocked back a serious amount of whisky, and he'd miss her. As wild, as reckless and as driven a woman as he'd ever met, he would miss her. She'd saved his life. He told her she needed to get out, needed to think about Frank, but she was in a quieter area of work, and she loved her arts.

They'd all left the hotel venue that night, jumped in taxis and come back to the station. Now they sat inside of Hope's office. There were a few bottles on the table, and Macleod was sitting on top of Hope's desk. The frivolity had gone, and there was a quietness now.

Macleod looked around. There was Hope in her jeans, a plain t-shirt. Sabine was dressed up, with an arm around Emmett. He, as usual, was wearing one of those t-shirts with some creature on it. Macleod had never really got to understand the man.

Perry was wearing a shirt. It was half hanging out now. Jona was sitting beside him. Susan was at the far end of the table with Ross beside her. He'd asked Jane to come back, but she hadn't come. She told him this was his time, his time to say goodbye to them all.

Patterson was looking dapper and was half supporting Clarissa. The Glasgow pair from the arts team had been up, but they'd headed back. He hadn't really got to know them, not that well, but they'd said goodbye. But these people in the room, this were his team. These were his people, nearly all of them. One was missing, but she'd gone off to a different life. He jumped down off the desk and looked around them all.

'I don't want to make a speech,' he said.

'But you will,' said Clarissa.

'You,' said Macleod, 'shush.' He held his finger up to his mouth as he looked about. He thought he was probably the only sober one in the room. Certainly, he was the only one who hadn't drunk anything.

'I just wanted to say before I went, thank you all. We've been through some tough times. I thought I'd lost you sometimes. Since I came up from Glasgow, Hope's been with me the longest, then Ross. Then we had wee Kirsten, and then the rest of you came on board, bit by bit. Some of you have saved my life. I watched Ross get shot. I've watched Hope been pummelled how many times. Clarissa pulled me out of the fire.

'You've looked after each other, and I don't look at my colleagues here. That's what I did when we were back at the party. Everybody there was my colleagues. And I would have bled for any of them. Decent people. You people here have been my family. I don't say things like this lightly, but I love you all deeply.

'Hope's going to run this murder team. She's got a few changes. Sabine's in with you now. And Susan's going across to work with Emmett. The place is in excellent hands. I won't sit and tell you that you'll have no problems, that everything will go smoothly, because it won't. It will be a mess at times. You'll get through; you'll get some tough cases that will break you. But you'll pick each other up and get on with it. You'll save each other. You might even lose the odd person on the way; I hope to God not. But you don't know what comes with this job.

'I just want to say thank you to you all. Thank you for all the gifts you gave me. Anyway, what I will say is, don't worry about me. I'm going on to something different. I'm going on to a life with Jane. When it comes to work, there's no other people I'd rather have been with. You are my family. Some of you will continue to be my family outside.' He looked at Hope. 'This one especially, with little Ian.

'Don't invite me back for Christmas. Don't invite me back to work. All of you are welcome to come and see me, but you come and see me as friends, never as ex-colleagues. I don't want to know about cases. If I'm needed because of past experience, fine, call me in. I'll come in, I'll interview, and I'll go. Treat me as a witness.

'But when you come to my house, you come as a friend. You come to ask about me, you come to tell me about your side of here. And if that means you bore me to death, Emmett, about some gaming convention, you come and you do it. If that means Clarissa, you come and tell me what Frank has shot recently around whatever course, or you come and talk to me about some piece of art I have no interest in, then you do it. But you always come as friends.

'Never again will you refer to me as DCI. I walk out of that door tonight. I am Seoras. And Ross, I swear to you that if you ever call me Macleod again, or sir, I will punch you. I will flatten you to the floor, and I will repeatedly hit you until I have knocked out this thing where you believe I am above you, am I clear?'

Ross nodded, and Macleod thought he could see a tear in his eye. He could feel himself beginning to choke. He turned and grabbed his cup, which currently had some coke in it. All the other glasses had something a little more alcoholic, but he raised his.

'To family,' he said. 'To family in the future and seeing my friends.'

Hope came over and tapped his glass, and the rest stood up. 'Family and friends,' went the refrain, and he drank his coke, fighting to keep the bubbles from making him burp.

'Go now,' he said. 'Come up one at a time and go. I don't want to walk away from you all. I want to leave here on my own tonight.'

Emmett and Sabine came up first. Emmett shook his hand, and Sabine gave him a hug. He wished them the best together and watched as they left. Perry came up next with Tanya. He hugged Tanya, thanking her for looking after him these last few months, and told Perry to take up the mantle, to be his man for Hope.

When they left, Susan came up. She hugged him and went to go, but he stopped her. 'Susan, I don't know how you'll recover from missing out on Perry, but you will find someone. You're too good. With Emmett, be yourself. Make a career.'

'You took me from nothing,' she said. 'I was the bike. I was the one that everybody wanted to screw. That's how they saw me. You never did.'

'There's a fighter in you. Similar to Hope. Not the same. But you've got a brain, like her. You're clever. Work hard. Emmett will appreciate you. He really will. But make sure you challenge him. It's time to shine,' said Macleod. 'I know when I pick them. I picked you because you're good. You can be the best.'

She hugged him and kissed him on the cheek. 'Thank you for everything,' she said.

He watched her leave, and this time felt a tear come down. Ross came over next, and he shook his hand. 'Thank you, sir,' said Ross. 'One last time, when I go through that door, and I will never call you it again.'

'And you'll always be Alan after this. But you've stood by me, Ross. Find what you want to be within the team. Help Hope, see what you are and be that. If a specialist, be a specialist. You're a remarkable man.' Macleod hugged him and then struggled to watch him go.

He turned and looked. Patterson came forward and shook his hand. Macleod told him to look after her, pointing at Clarissa. Patterson nodded. 'It's been an honour,' he said. 'I'll wait outside for her. Get her home.'

'You better do or Frank will never forgive me,' said Macleod. He smiled and then watched as Clarissa came up to him.

'I wanted to buy you a shawl,' she said. 'A good tartan one, to keep you warm. She's a lucky woman.' She threw her arms around him, pulling him in tight.

'We damn well near lost you too many times,' said Clarissa.

'You brought me onto this team. I didn't need to be among the murders. It hurt me.'

'I know,' said Macleod, 'and I'm sorry. I'm sorry I brought you onto the team. It was a bad call. You're where you need to be now. It's where you're good.'

'But I don't regret coming for you,' she said. 'You lovely man.' She kissed him on the forehead. 'Don't be a stranger to me either,' she said. 'Frank says you're welcome anytime. We'll see you, Seoras.'

She turned and walked away, leaving only Hope in the room. Macleod looked at her. Hope was wearing her hair in a ponytail, and tears were streaming down her face.

'You'll see me again. You'll see me a lot. That kid of yours.'

'I know, but this is goodbye to my boss,' she said. 'You've always been my boss. I've fought with you at times. You've been wrong and I've corrected you. You've helped me too. This, whatever comes next, it won't be the same.'

'No, it won't. But I had others before you,' said Macleod. 'Others I've left behind along the way. Good people. Perry came back. You won't have all of this team forever. You'll say goodbye. Move on. We both said goodbye to Kirsten. People come and go. Life never stays the same. We only get one shot,' said Macleod. 'And I'm glad he was ill that day.'

'Who?'

'My sergeant in Glasgow. He was ill, and you had to come with me to Lewis. I still remember it. I still remember looking at you, and I remember what I thought. And I'm sorry for that. I thought God was dumping a brazen woman on me. Instead, he's given me one of the best friends I've ever had.'

Hope stepped forward and hugged him. 'I felt something that first day,' said Hope. 'John's lucky you weren't twenty years younger, or maybe thirty.'

'We'd have been bad for each other,' said Macleod. 'Don't even think about that. You've got a great man, and I've got a woman who needs me, who understands me, and will see me through this retirement. But I will miss McGrath, even though I still have Hope.'

'And you're leaving,' she said. 'This is my office, and I will leave it in a bit. But I am not walking out now to be met by the rest of them. I told them all they had to go. On your terms, I let you leave here, saying goodbye, without anybody else. I need a moment before I go back to John. And I'll do it in my office, because this is my office now.'

'Yes, it is. I'll see you soon,' said Macleod. He walked to the door and stopped and turned to look at her. 'Don't let them take you out of here. Don't let them take you away from the chase. It's where you and I are the same. It lives in you like it lives in me still. But the body can't take it anymore. This is where you belong. Don't forget it.'

He turned, looked for his new fedora hat and put it on his head. He wrapped himself up in a coat, and then he pulled the tie that he was wearing. He turned and threw it into the office.

'This stays here,' he said. 'Hang it, put it in a cupboard, do something with it. I walk out of here, Seoras. Not Macleod.'

Hope smiled at him, tears in her eyes. And Macleod turned and walked. He went down the stairs. There were a few people there. Some waved and said goodbye. Others let him be because he was clearly in his own thoughts. He got outside and went to walk to his car. He'd left it there to drive himself back, but as he approached it he thought he heard something. Macleod stopped and looked up. There was a figure there in a black leather jacket, with long black hair. She was shorter than he was.

'So this is it,' Anna Hunt said. 'So what is it now? Do I call you Inspector? Do I call you Macleod? What do I call you?'

'Seoras,' he said. 'I left Detective Chief Inspector Macleod up there. See, no tie.'

'I thought I should drop by just to say thank you on behalf of the Service. You helped us at different times, and I just wanted to say goodbye myself.'

Macleod stepped forward, extending a hand. 'You've helped a great deal. You saved some of my colleagues, kept them safe, my friends. Thank you.' He bent forward and kissed her on the cheek.

'You really left him up there, didn't you?'

'Jane says I've got to be warmer now. Got to embrace a new me. A me that's got to live life and see it differently.'

'She's not wrong there. Go to her. I hope you enjoy your life. Make the most of it.'

'Keep safe,' said Macleod, 'and thank you. I guess very few people ever tell you that.'

He watched her smile before he got into the car. Driving away, he felt a tear or two in his eye, leaving the station for the last time. He was crossing the bridge towards Kessock when he heard the noise in the back seat of the car.

'You can pull in at the car park at the Kessock bridge.'

He pulled in, stopped and got out of the car, by which time his passenger had left the back seat. She was in her leather jacket, black jeans, and she threw her arms around him.

'You don't think I'd let you quit like that?'

'Will you come back to the house?'

'No. But I won't be a stranger. I wanted to tell you that. I'll pop in and see you.'

'You were one of the best things I did in this job,' said Macleod. 'You, Hope. The both of you. You, the rest of the team. You were, you were everything. Until you went off and—'

'You looked after my brother. You did so much for me. Enjoy retirement. Be in retirement and don't come back to any of this. If you need me, at any point, here,' she said, slipping a mobile phone into his pocket. 'The number's on there. You ring it. I will come. If you have any trouble from your past or your future, I will be there. But I will come every now and again to make sure you are taking care of yourself.' He hugged her tight.

It differed from Hope. He knew he would see Hope soon. Hope was going to be part of his life in the future. He wasn't sure how much he would see of Kirsten, and yet she'd been such a favourite of his. Wiping his eyes, he got back in the car. He watched the rear-view mirror as she stood, knowing she'd be gone if he turned around. That's how she was.

By the time he had reached his house and parked the car, he thought he would quietly get it into the house and not disturb Jane. She was standing in her dressing gown on the front doorstep.

'Did it go okay?' she asked.

'I left him,' he said. 'No tie, I left him. I left him in the office with Hope. And Kirsten came.'

He threw his arms around her. He cried, and he kept crying on the step. After about five minutes, he stopped and looked up. 'I'm ready,' he said. 'I've left him. It's time for us. It's time for our future, Seoras and Jane. I'm yours, all yours.'

A Wee Word From the Author

It's been fifty books with Macleod, starting with a punt to nothing, my first crime novel. He's grown along with my writing, given me a writing career and a readership I deeply appreciate. Thank you if you have made it all the way through all fifty books. I hope you enjoyed the ride!

The Highlands and Islands Detective Thriller Series is not done, and Hope and the team will return in "Lonely at the Top", book 51. Macleod, or should I say, Seoras, is not done either. Along with Jane, he will find crime doesn't reside purely in Scotland. "Seoras, They Shot Him!" starts his new adventures which I hope you will all read and enjoy.

As Macleod said, "Life never stays the same. We only get one shot." Here's to the next novels!

Read on to discover the Patrick Smythe series!

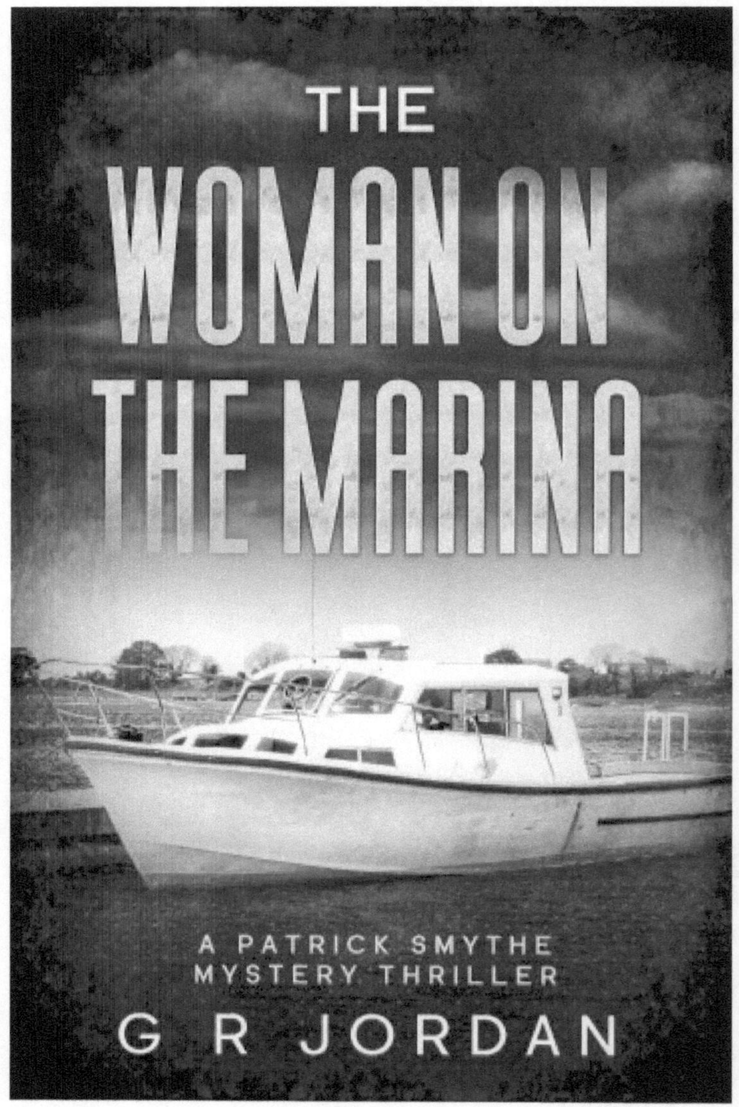
THE
WOMAN ON
THE MARINA
A PATRICK SMYTHE
MYSTERY THRILLER
G R JORDAN

Patrick Smythe is a former Northern Irish policeman who after suffering an amputation after a bomb blast, takes to the sea between the west coast of Scotland and his homeland to ply his trade as a private investigator. Join Paddy as he tries to work to his own ethics while knowing how to bend the rules he once enforced. Working from his beloved motorboat 'Craigantlet', Paddy decides to rescue a drug mule in this short story from the pen of G R Jordan.

Join G R Jordan's monthly newsletter about forthcoming releases and special writings for his tribe of avid readers and then receive your free Patrick Smythe short story.

Go to https://bit.ly/PatrickSmythe for your Patrick Smythe journey to start.

About the Author

GR Jordan is a self-published author who finally decided at forty that in order to have an enjoyable lifestyle, his creative beast within would have to be unleashed. His books mirror that conflict in life where acts of decency contend with self-promotion, goodness stares in horror at evil, and kindness blindsides us when we at our worst. Corrupting our world with his parade of wondrous and horrific characters, he highlights everyday tensions with fresh eyes whilst taking his methodical, intelligent mainstays on a roller-coaster ride of dilemmas, all the while suffering the banter of their provocative sidekicks.

A graduate of Loughborough University where he masqueraded as a chemical engineer but ultimately played American football, Gary had worked at changing the shape of cereal flakes and pulled a pallet truck for a living. Watching vegetables freeze at -40'C was another career highlight and he was also one of the Scottish Highlands "blind" air traffic controllers.

These days he has graduated to answering a telephone to people in trouble before telephoning other people to sort it out.

Having flirted with most places in the UK, he is now based in the Isle of Lewis in Scotland where his free time is spent between raising a young family with his wife, writing, figuring out how to work a loom and caring for a small flock of chickens. Luckily, his writing is influenced by his varied work and life experience as the chickens have not been the poetical inspiration he had hoped for!

You can connect with me on:

🌐 https://www.grjordan.com

f https://facebook.com/carpetlessleprechaun

Subscribe to my newsletter:

✉ https://bit.ly/PatrickSmythe

Also by G R Jordan

G R Jordan writes across multiple genres including crime, dark and action adventure fantasy, feel good fantasy, mystery thriller and horror fantasy. Below is a selection of his work. Whilst all books are available across online stores, signed copies are available at his personal shop.

Seoras, They Shot Him! (Seoras Macleod Mysteries #1)
https://grjordan.com/product/seoras-1
Sun, sea…and a mystery thicker than suncream!

When former DCI Seoras Macleod and his bubbly partner Jane set off for a promised fortnight of bliss on a glittering private island—white sand beaches, luxury huts, and endless sunshine—what could possibly go wrong? But paradise curdles when Jane, out on a solitary walk, glimpses an argument on the far side of the island's restricted compound—and what looks horrifyingly like an execution. Was it a trick of the heat, or something far more sinister?

Retirement was only an excuse to start working together!

Lonely at the Top (Highlands & Islands Detective Thrillers #51)

https://grjordan.com/product/lonely-at-the-top

An elite businessman is found dead at the top of the Cairngorms. A solitary life leads to no clues about a motive. In her first case after Macleod's retirement can Hope deliver as her new DCI questions if she really can cut the mustard?

In the wake of DCI Macleod's retirement, DI Hope McGrath inherits a new DCI, one who doesn't hold with the glamourous image Hope has within the force. When a man without enemies is brutally killed atop the Cairngorms, Hope feels the pressure as she is harangued over every move she makes by her new boss. With her young boy pining for Mum, and her partner struggling at home, can Hope rise above the distractions and pressure to understand who wants the perfect hermit dead?

The quiet life is merely turbulence in the shadows!

Kirsten Stewart Thrillers
https://grjordan.com/product/a-shot-at-democracy

Join Kirsten Stewart on a shadowy ride through the underbelly of the Highlands of Scotland where among the beauty and splendour of the majestic landscape lies corruption and intrigue to match any city. From murders to extortion, missing children to criminals operating above the law, the Highland former detective must learn a tougher edge to her work as she puts her own life on the line to protect those who cannot defend themselves.

Having left her beloved murder investigation team far behind, Kirsten has to battle personal tragedy and loss while adapting to a whole new way of executing her duties where your mistakes are your own. As Kirsten comes to terms with working with the new team, she often operates as the groups solo field agent, placing herself in danger and trouble to rescue those caught on the dark side of life. With action packed scenes and tense scenarios of murder and greed, the Kirsten Stewart thrillers will have you turning page after page to see your favourite Scottish lass home!

There's life after Macleod, but a whole new world of death!

Jac's Revenge (A Jac Moonshine Thriller #1)

https://grjordan.com/product/jacs-revenge

An unexpected hit makes Debbie a widow. The attention of her man's killer spawns a brutal yet classy alter ego. But how far can you play the game before it takes over your life?

All her life, Debbie Parlor lived in her man's shadow, knowing his work was never truly honest. She turned her head from news stories and rumours. But when he was disposed of for his smile to placate a rival crime lord, Jac Moonshine was born. And when Debbie is paid compensation for her loss like her car was written off, Jac decides that enough is enough.

Get on board with this tongue-in-cheek revenge thriller that will make you question how far you would go to avenge a loved one, and how much you would enjoy it!

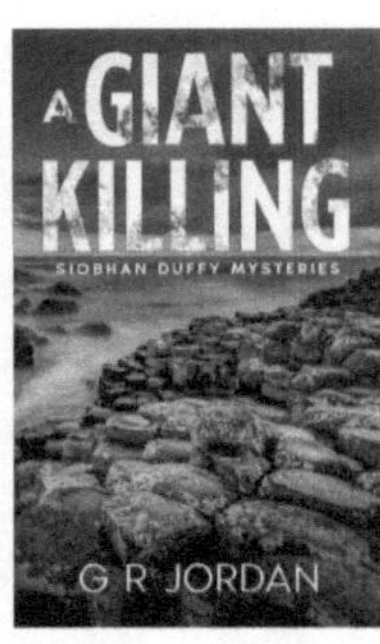

A Giant Killing (Siobhan Duffy Mysteries #1)
https://grjordan.com/product/a-giant-killing
A body lies on the Giant's boot. Discord, as the master of secrets has been found. Can former spy Siobhan Duffy find the killer before they execute her former colleagues?

When retired operative Siobhan Duffy sees the killing of her former master in the paper, her unease sends her down a path of discovery and fear. Aided by her young housekeeper and scruff of a gardener, Siobhan begins a quest to discover the reason for her spy boss' death and unravels a can of worms today's masters would rather keep closed. But in a world of secrets, the difference between revenge and simple, if brutal, housekeeping becomes the hardest truth to know.

The past is a child who never leaves home!